# THE BLUE MAN

# THE BLUE MAN

## A Door Opens to Worlds Beyond

SUE LUMB

BROWN DOG BOOKS

First published 2021



Published under licence by Brown Dog Books and
The Self-Publishing Partnership Ltd, 10b Greenway Farm, Bath Rd, Wick, nr. Bath BS30 5RL

www.selfpublishingpartnership.co.uk

ISBN printed book: 978-1-83952-345-8
ISBN e-book: 978-1-83952-346-5

Cover design by Kevin Rylands
Internal design by Andrew Easton

Printed and bound in the UK

This book is printed on FSC certified paper

MIX
Paper from responsible sources
FSC® C013604
www.fsc.org

*I would like to dedicate my book to my family, Pete, Dan, Kate and Zac who are an inspiration for everything that is wonderful.*

# THE STORM

At first light the *Gothenburg Star* sailed from the port of Stockholm. Yan, a student from the university, had secured a passage joining the crew as a marine researcher. As the ship steamed ahead he gripped the rail on the side of the ship and looked back to the port. He felt excited and anxious. This would be his last opportunity to gather further evidence to support his thesis about unusual seismic activity in the Celtic Sea. He needed more data to corroborate his theory about the effects this was having on the marine ecology of the area. He would submit his findings to the university as part of his PhD. If the Science Institute validated his findings he would be awarded a bursary to continue his research.

He felt the cold chill of the wind in his face and looked out across the water as the glow from the harbour lights drifted into the distant horizon. He could feel the low vibration of the engine as it began to get into its stride. The conditions were perfect. The ship seemed to coast along effortlessly. In no time at all he realised he had nearly completed his first watch and he was relieved that all seemed to have gone well.

Over the next few days, the ship's voyage wound away from Sweden, around the Skagerrak, south into the busy shipping lanes of the English Channel, and finally turned north into the Celtic Sea. After an afternoon of study in his cabin, Yan wandered down to the stern of the ship to check the monitors and log the first set of readings. So far, everything appeared normal.

He was about to head back to his cabin when the ship suddenly lurched to one side. This was so unexpected that he lost his balance and he fell against a large wooden box, gashing the side of his head as he did so. He was alarmed by the amount of blood which was oozing from the wound. As he tried to stem the bleeding, he looked up and saw that the crew were frantically tying off ropes and gear that had come loose. He stumbled towards the door, holding his hand against his forehead. Blood was dripping down his face and onto his collar. He found it hard to keep his balance. Someone shouted to him, 'Get yourself inside, that cut looks nasty!'

There seemed to be a lot of agitated activity as they pulled on the flapping tarpaulins which secured the cargo. The captain had ordered a full alert. He was on the bridge and looked anxious. He had received an urgent weather report informing him of the conditions above Fastnet. Apparently, it was gale force 10 and rising, and the storm was heading straight for them. A voice rang out, 'All hands on deck!'

Yan turned and tried to make his way along the side of the ship. He could hear lots of shouting as more commands were being hurled at the crew. They too were taken aback by the immediacy of the storm that seemed to come out of nowhere.

Waves began to heap up. In the unforgiving swell, the ship began rocking violently from side to side. He could see that the clouds were getting darker and more menacing.

The ship began to veer repeatedly off course as the waves crashed across its path. The storm was so fierce that they could not escape it, and had no choice but to ride it out. Hours passed as the ship was tossed to and fro, helpless against such forces.

On the bridge the navigator drew the captain's attention to the depth sounder. There seemed to be a dark shadow on the screen. At the same time a seismic monitor went off the scale. The captain sounded the alarm. Seven blasts were followed by one long one; the air was filled with a sense of fear and panic. Huge waves were swamping the decks and it was impossible for the ship to make headway. A distress signal was sent out, and crew were sent to muster stations, donning life jackets in readiness. As the roll call was checked, it was discovered that there was a man overboard. On discovering this, the crew frantically tried to locate the missing person.

A flare was set off which illuminated the sea just beyond the stern of the ship. A beacon scoured the rolling waves. The boat was tossing back and forth and waves were pounding the deck, the captain muttered, 'I've never seen anything like this before.'

He called the first mate to begin the evacuation.

'We're not gonna make it, how far from land are we?'

The navigator tried to assess their position, but it was impossible to make out the coordinates.

'Look, there's a light flashing in the distance!'

It was a beam from a lighthouse. They seemed to be approaching some kind of reef.

'We're taking on too much water. It's gonna take a miracle to get us out of this.'

Then there was an enormous grinding roar as the hull of the ship hit the edge of the reef. They began the emergency procedures and were about to launch the lifeboats when out of nowhere the shape of a boat could be seen. It was racing towards them all lights aglare and it became clear that it was a lifeboat.

'Where the hell did that come from?' someone shouted.

It had launched from Port Lar on the Isle of Manes, which they had been driven towards in the storm. The coastguard had spotted their flare and the lifeboat crew responded as soon as they heard the siren, racing to the lifeboat station from all over the island. Drilled in such an emergency, they were at their posts in no time at all.

'It's going to be a tricky shout,' said Frank, the boatswain.

The lifeboat berthed its way down the slipway and into the powerful swell of the unforgiving sea. Fortunately the vessel was sturdy and powerful, and it ploughed its way head on through the towering and unrelenting seas. Very quickly they came alongside the stricken vessel. As soon as they were alerted to the fact that a man was overboard, their searchlights scoured the waves.

'I think I can see something,' shouted Frank, who was pointing to a shape in the water. They edged closer to where he was pointing and sure enough there was someone floating with his head just visible above the waves.

'Pass me the hook, I think I can get him.'

They hurled a lifebelt into the sea and the man grabbed it. It was Yan. He reached with all his might and managed to put the lifebelt over his head. Frank then leaned over the side and hauled him ungraciously in. He lay comatose on the deck. Another five minutes and he would have drowned.

Yan had lost his balance when the ship swung around. Despite his efforts to hold on to the rail, the force of the surge had propelled him over the side.

As he began to recover, all he could remember was falling into the sea and the icy shock of the water overwhelming him. He recalled sinking beneath the waves and being overcome by a sense of panic as a strange bluish shape had emerged from the depths. He remembered its long undulating body swimming towards him.

The creature had fixed a mesmerising gaze on him. For a moment he was transfixed and time seemed to stop. His mind seemed to be filled with strange images, both familiar and surreal. He saw himself as a child and for instance relived the grief of losing his parents in a tragic accident. Strangely, he heard them cry out and felt the force of the impact of the car which had hit them. He felt himself being lifted from the wreckage. He remembered feeling confused and scared. He then began to see himself as an older child, riding along the path on his bike by the side of his grandmother's house. 'Buster', the old faithful Labrador, was following him. He remembered his school, and playing football with his friends in the school yard. Then all went black as the activities of the lifeboat above seemed to dispel the blue shape, which then dissipated into the murky depths.

Somehow, he found himself above the water reaching out towards a life belt which had been thrown to him. He heard a man shouting. It was Frank.

'Got ya ... ya bloody idiot what do you think ya doing in the water, you'll catch yer death.' As he hit the deck he could feel his lungs burning. His body heaved as he vomited and then he began to slowly recover. He was wrapped in blankets and given a warm drink. 'You were bloody lucky, mate,' the voice was unfamiliar but comforting.

The lifeboat sped back through the heaving waves into the harbour of Port Lar. Port Lar village lay nestled between the green hills of Barullane and the Manes Sea. It was a pretty little place, a throwback, removed as it was from the rest of the world.

It consisted of rows of precariously built, white stone cottages which cascaded down chalky cliffs, at the bottom of which was a bustling harbour filled with an array of fishing boats.

The storm had come in from nowhere, forcing the fishermen to abandon mending their nets and secure all the lobster pots on the quay side. They moved to take refuge in an old ramshackle hut at the top of the cliff. As they fought their way against the wind, they could hear the roar of the huge waves crashing over the harbour wall, and saw blankets of white froth swirling around in the fearsome wind.

There was a great sense of relief when the lifeboat was spotted making its return. As it docked it could still be seen bobbing up and down in the unyielding and ferocious swell. The lifeboat crew disembarked swiftly along the heaving gangway followed by the men from the *Gothenburg,* who had had to abandon ship. They clung to each other as they were beckoned along. They were cold, tired and hungry, but nonetheless relieved to have survived.

Once ashore they were led to the harbour office.

'That must have been a tricky shout, George,' said the duty officer.

George swelled with pride and replied, 'Got a good team.'

'Well I guess it'll be your round then!' shouted Frank, as he followed behind. There was silence, George grimaced and then laughed.

'Not one to miss a trick, eh!' Frank looked sheepish.

They swaggered along the pier to a scruffy looking establishment at the end of the quay. It was called 'the Fisherman's Arms'. On the outside wall hung a weather-beaten figurehead of a blue-headed woman, beneath which there was a noticeboard which swung on two rusty hinges, it read 'Round island trip to see the seals and caves of Emnerald Rocks'. The spelling of 'Emerald' was noticeably not quite right.

# ISLAND LIFE

Some of the fishermen worked shifts on the lifeboat as well as running fishing boat tours around the Emerald Rocks. Frank knew the sea around there well, it was quite treacherous with the swirling tides and its strange turbulent eddies. Fortunately for Yan, Frank had been on duty when the *Gothenburg* had gone aground on the rocks.

The 'Fisherman's Arms' was the most popular pub. It was the centre of the community. The proprietor was known as 'Uncle George'. He wore several hats. He was also the skipper of the lifeboat, a fireman and the local councillor. He was relieved that when he had to attend that night's 'shout', he was able to rely on his niece Grace to stand in for Ruth, the regular barmaid, who had been unavoidably delayed.

He had called her mobile when he had heard the lifeboat siren. He knew he had to get to the lifeboat station as fast as he could. Every second counted in such emergencies.

'Gracie, I know it's a lot to ask and it's a filthy night but could you possibly do a shift tonight? We've got a call out. There's been some flooding at the Beck and Ruth says she's stuck, I'll make it up to you.'

'Of course, no problem, I'll just go and drop my stuff off at the house.'

'You're a star, my favourite niece. I'll catch you later.'

Fortunately for him, she had agreed to do the shift, even though she felt quite exhausted having worked all day at the local garden centre.

Grace and her mother lived at 'Dove' cottage, just above the quay, about five minutes from the Fisherman's Arms. Grace was living on her student grant and was grateful for occasional bar work to supplement her income. She was training to be a horticulturist. She had always liked working outdoors. Being knowledgeable about various plant species and habitats and being part of the process of cultivating seeds to flower gave her immense satisfaction.

She was presently doing work experience at the local garden centre. Her task was to establish some lily plants in the water garden. She wanted to impress the manager and had been working tirelessly all day. To be asked to do a night behind the bar was the last thing she wanted to do, but her uncle had seemed quite desperate, so she felt obliged to help out.

On such a stormy night it was hard to resist the cosy comforts of her mother's cottage, the sweet smell of pine logs burning on the stove, the tempting smell of home cooking and the sofa, which seemed to be beckoning her to collapse into its soft voluminous embrace. Her mum, who had been busy in the kitchen, began to grumble about Uncle George.

'He's got a nerve asking you to go out on such a horrible night.'

'Don't worry, Mum, I could do with the extra cash.'

'Well, I suppose he's had a lot of problems recently. You know I could ring that other barmaid's neck, what a little madam she was, and poor Frank!'

The new barmaid that George had hired recently had caused quite a scandal in the village and everyone had something to say about it.

'Mum, not now, I've got to go.'

She grabbed her coat and headed down the lane on her bike. She was cold and drenched by the time she reached the pub. The siren could still be heard ringing out across the village.

'Oh no! That sea looks really rough,' she thought to herself.

The storm was very much in evidence as the wind howled and dark ominous clouds gathered overhead. Uncle George drove past her in his beaten up old Volkswagen saying, 'Could anything else go wrong tonight? Thanks love, see you later.'

On her arrival at the pub old Charlie was propped up in the cubby hole as usual.

'I've never seen it so rough, look at the lightning. It must be force 11 veering over the Emerald Rocks, that's not good.'

Old Charlie dragged on his 'roly'. Smoke billowed above him. He was playing dominoes as usual, clicking the little tiles in his hand and then deftly moving them around the table. Several dead matches were sticking out of the scoring block. It seemed he had a winning round, but he looked anxious.

Old Charlie then got up and looked out through the great bay window at the sea. He began to shake his head and started a running commentary about what he could see. The rest of the clientele listened intently.

'There's another flare, someone must be in the water.

Dunno what that boat could be that they are racing up to, but it's pitching all over the place. Must be one of those northern boats ... ah! Someone must have been picked up,' there was a tense pause, 'they are towing the boat back, yes ... they are on their way back ... better get those pumps ready, Gracie.'

Grace had a sinking feeling as she realised that she would have to manage a very busy pub by herself.

An hour or so later there was a lot of commotion as the crew piled into the place. It began to reek of steaming oilskins and sweaty rubber boots which were thrown in a heap near the fire.

She was relieved that her uncle had got back safely, although she wasn't expecting him to bring the crew back from another ship. She knew it was going to be a long night.

'That was a close call,' said George as he turned to Frank.

'You did well, son, he owes his life to you.'

He pointed at the stranger who was hunched in the corner looking very sorry for himself. Frank smiled, he was glad to have done something right.

Frank looked up to George. George had been a very close friend of his father, who had tragically drowned ten years previously. His boat had been stricken by a fearsome storm. He was the last man on board as it went down. The lifeboat crew had been unable to reach him. It had been a terrible tragedy that had left its mark on George. Poor Frank was just a small boy when it happened. So, George felt it was his moral duty to look out for him.

It was a foregone conclusion that Frank would follow in his father's footsteps. It was his family that owned the most prominent fleet on the island. It was assumed he would take control of the family business, although he had other dreams and didn't want the responsibility.

He wasn't business minded either, being more interested in where all the action was. At every opportunity he would take off to sea and when ashore would most likely be found tinkering with a boat that he was renovating. His ambition was to sail single handed across the Atlantic. The sea was in his blood. He was by all accounts a natural seafarer and had already gained a wide knowledge of the nature of the sea. He knew both the joys and the dangers of its embrace.

It was unfortunate that his youth and folly eventually led him into a storm of a different nature. George had felt somewhat responsible. It all began when he had hired a young attractive barmaid to cover Ruth's maternity leave. Ruth was the regular barmaid and Frank's older sister. Little did he know the problems this would cause. The new barmaid, Maisie, appeared to be hardworking but underneath the charming exterior was a determination to better herself one way or another. She had no intention of pulling pints for the rest of her life.

Her weapon was her skill to flatter, which she utilised with unashamed confidence. She lured men easily with her charms. It was unfortunate that she had her sights set on young Frank and of course his promising financial prospects.

'That Maisie was a bad 'un, you were best rid of her,' said Charlie

Frank sank into his chair and stared blankly at the wall, he didn't want another inquisition about Maisie as he was tired and irritated. Charlie then ambled over to the bar where Grace was busy washing glasses. Grace turned to her uncle and rolled her eyes as she had heard the story too many times.

'Oh leave him alone, he's had a tough call.'

Frank had an ambivalent expression on his face; he just wanted to have a pint and go home. His moment of peace was soon shattered as little Jimmy, his son, was spotted wailing at the door. He looked dirty and unkempt with a snotty nose. He wasn't a pleasant looking child. Frank's sister Ruth had finally turned up. She had been stuck at Briars Hill with her young baby, who had vomited all over her, and young Jimmy who followed her into the pub. She was tired, agitated and full of apologies.

'Sorry George, the car got stuck.' She turned to Grace.

'Sorry Grace. She turned to Frank. 'Sorry Frank, the stormy weather always upsets him.' 'No bother, I'm on my way home, come to daddy, son.'

The child gladly hurled himself towards Frank, who then slung him over his shoulder and left.

'Frank's lucky to have you as a sister,' said Uncle George.

Ruth just smiled and said, 'We all know he's had a difficult time, let's just let him get on with life.'

Then Charlie piped up, 'Still can't believe what happened to young Frank. He used to be so different, always laughing and joking.'

'Yes we all know that woman got her claws into our Frank that night. I hope the poor bugger she ran off with gets what's coming to him.'

At that remark one of the crew members shouted out, 'Yeah, Maisie certainly had talents,' and he laughed.

'Right, you can be quiet. Frank's back now and shall we just leave it at that,' she disappeared behind the bar to help Grace with the pumps.

Maisie had worked out that Frank would be the best catch, being the only male heir to what was a wealthy family business. Her opportunity to reel him in happened at his twenty-first birthday bash. In his inebriated state he was egged on by his mates, but this time things went too far.

'Hey Maisie, how about giving Frankie a birthday kiss.'

Maisie had stepped out from behind the bar saying, 'Come to Maisie, Frankie boy, if you dare?'

Having downed several pints, he had willingly succumbed to her lusty embrace. He was no match for her womanly charms and later that night she gained her opportunity to snare him. The seed was sown. Keen to do the right thing on learning of her pregnancy, Frank was forced into a hapless marriage. To his credit, he tried to make a go of it and they muddled along together for a while, but the relationship was fated from the start. He concentrated less and less on the fishing business, which was already falling into decline and was not bringing in the rewards that Maisie had hoped for. The consequence now being that Frank found himself bearing the burden of bringing up their offspring Jimmy by himself, because Maisie had soon given up on maternal responsibility.

She began to spend more and more time in the pub, ingratiating herself to any willing suitor. It wasn't long before she took a fancy to a salesman from Christchurch, and in no time at all just packed her things and disappeared. Everyone felt that Frank and young Jimmy had been treated quite ruthlessly.

Fortunately, Frank's sister Ruth was adept at getting him out of tight spots. Although his situation seemed hopeless, she had had an idea. She had spotted a job in the local paper that she thought would temporarily offer him some respite. She felt he desperately needed to sort himself out. A short phone call seemed to do the trick.

'Hi Frankie, Ruth here, remember you said you wanted to try your luck on the trawlers?'

'Yes, why?'

'Well, I've just had a look in the paper, there's an opportunity for you. They need someone straight away, with experience, and it would be good money.'

'Sounds good but I can't, what about Jimmy?' He knew she was trying to help but he couldn't see how.

However, Ruth wasn't going to take 'no' for an answer and quickly replied 'You can leave little Jimmy with me. It's not like you are going to be away forever!'

A Danish fishing trawler was scouting for a crew. The vessel in question was bound for the North Sea. Experienced fishermen were needed for the season. Frank got the number of the agent and made an application. He had all the necessary credentials and was accepted straight away. He was a little apprehensive about leaving young Jimmy, but he consoled himself with the fact that he would be well cared for by his sister and he desperately needed the money. At this point in his life he knew he had nothing to lose. He rang his sister to tell her his news. She was delighted. 'Brilliant, I'm really pleased for you, Frank. Remember, if it doesn't work out, just come back. Things will work out one way or another.'

'Thanks, sis, I promise I'll make it up to you.' He was still unsure but he had decided to take her up on the offer. It was the break he needed. Within a week he was gone.

He spent most of that winter at sea hauling catches in the harsh conditions of the North Sea. The arduous physical work seemed to help him to forget the events of the last few years. However, he hadn't bargained for the desperate feeling of isolation. He missed Port Lar desperately.

One night as he lay tossing and turning in his bunk there was a face which he just couldn't get out of his mind, that of Grace, who had always been his secret passion. They had grown up together and she had always had time for him. He had felt somewhat in awe of her and had never dared pluck up the courage to tell her his feelings. He believed that his dalliance with Maisie had ruined any chance of a relationship, but still he couldn't get her out of his mind. He knew he would have to go back. When the last haul of the season had finished he handed in his notice and left.

The day he returned to Manes he was greeted by old Charlie, who was sitting on the side of the pier.

'Suppose it didn't work out then.'

'No!' was Frank's abrupt reply as he marched homeward.

Back at the pub, time passed slowly for Grace as she attended to the thirsty crew. She yawned as she stared at the clock. It would be a 'lock in' and the beer continued to flow. She just wanted the evening to end. Old Jack seemed more oiled than the rest and began his usual unwelcome advances.

He put his heavy arm around her shoulders.

'Will you just get off me you old goat!' She was adept at wrestling herself away from him.

It was at that point she saw a stranger staring at her. It was Yan. He'd followed the crew to the pub. He was still in shock and was shivering. He was sitting by the warming embers of the fire trying to make sense of it all.

As he looked at her he felt she was like an oasis of calm amidst all the noise and confusion. He noticed her deep soulful eyes, there was something very beguiling about her. He caught her glance. She decided to get a closer look, and began clearing glasses from a nearby table. She could see he was feeling the cold. She picked up a coat and put it around his shoulders. 'You look like you have seen a ghost. She was concerned.

'I don't feel well,' he replied in broken English.

His head began to droop and she felt the heavy weight of his body in her arms.

'Oh my God, hold on, I'll get help,' she gestured to one of the crew, who rushed over.

'What have you done to him?' said Uncle George, who tried to make light of the situation. It was then that Yan suddenly felt very weak, and was overcome by a strange disassociation and lost consciousness.

They called for an ambulance. As he lay in her arms she held him tightly. She could see there had been a nasty gash on his forehead. She wiped the dried blood from the side of his face. She didn't want to let go of him. It was a strange feeling. There was something about the stranger. It was a magnetic and immediate attraction. As his head rolled against her shoulder, she stroked his blonde hair, which was matted with dried blood. He was slightly built but quite tall. His angular features were typically Scandinavian and he must have been only in his late twenties. She noticed his long slender hands and thought it was very unlikely that he had done any hard physical work.

The ambulance arrived and whisked him away to the hospital in Christchurch.

It was not until several days later that she came into contact with him again. It happened while she was working at the garden centre. She was pulling weeds from the lily pond when she almost fell over as she reached for the new batch of seedlings, which she had placed on the muddy bank. A voice startled her.

'Hello, be careful, you might slip!'

He was standing directly behind her and had seen that the tray of seedlings were a little out of her reach.

'Here, let me pass them to you,' he leaned forward and she took the tray from him.

'Thanks, yes I'm already covered in mud.' She stared at him. 'Oh my goodness, you're the man from the pub, how are you feeling?'

'Much better thanks, seems I was concussed. Is that a Nymphaeaceae?'

'Yes, yes it's rhizomatous. Are you interested in plants?'

'Yes, in Sweden I was doing a lot of research into plants and gastropods as part of my PhD.'

She had to listen carefully to each word, as he spoke with a clipped Swedish accent. She interrupted him, 'But what were you doing on the ship?'

'Oh!, yes, I'm doing some research, marine ecology and seismology.'

'Well, you seemed to have certainly encountered some fierce weather. What are you doing here?'

'There was a lot of damage to the ship when it crashed

into the rocks, so the university is extending my stay so that I can repair some of the instruments. I am going to be hanging around here for a couple of weeks.'

'Oh! you are a student, that explains everything. Yes, there are lots of wrecks around there. My uncle was on the lifeboat that night; it's a dangerous place, you were lucky to survive.'

'Yes, I am very grateful to him and I think you too.' He smiled bashfully.

'No problem, glad to have been able to help. Well, if you are going to be here for a while, I could show you around, I'm Grace.' She smiled at him.

'Oh, yes I would like that, I'm Yan.' He smiled back,'

'Where are you staying?'

'I've got a room at the Fisherman's Arms,' he paused for a moment and caught her stare. 'Why don't you meet me there tonight, then you can tell me all about yourself.'

'Okay, it's a date!' She wasn't sure why she said that and why she formally shook his hand, but he seemed to look more cheerful.

After work, Grace rushed home, gulped down her tea and quickly got ready to go out again. Her mother called to her and jokingly said, 'You wouldn't by any chance be off to see that young man would you?'

'Ah, shut up, Mother, it's nothing. I'm just keeping him company for a while.'

'Oh! is that what you call it,' she laughed, but was pleased that Grace was beginning to enjoy herself.

When Grace arrived at the Fisherman's Arms she found Yan sitting in the cubby hole looking out to sea. She sat next to him and could see he was just staring out at the rocks.

'Well the sea looks much calmer now, doesn't it,' She caught his attention.

'Yes, much calmer.' He was pleased to see her.

'What will you do when you go back?' she asked

'Well, I will have to explain what happened that night and make an analysis of the findings from the instruments.' He looked apprehensive.

'Don't worry, you can tell them about the Blue Man!' she laughed

'What do you mean "Blue Man"?' he looked agitated

'Just joking! Everyone around here knows about them.'

He looked ashen. 'I don't understand, what do you mean? Don't make fun of me like that.' He became quite agitated.

'Sorry, I wasn't making fun of you, it's just a legend!'

She curled her lip and there was an awkward silence. She didn't want them to fall out. 'This place is full of weird stuff, legends and strange things in the sea, it's just fisherman talk!' She tried to make light of it all.

'Yes, sorry forgive my rudeness, I didn't mean anything. But I am interested in those legends you were talking about.'

'Ok, you are forgiven.' She smiled, then she had an idea.

'How about tomorrow we go to the library? My aunt is the librarian. There's a whole section on local myths, legends and stories. I need to get a couple of books myself, for my essay.'

He began to look a little more cheerful, but there was something in his expression she couldn't explain.

'Perhaps we could go for a walk afterwards along the prom?'

'Yes, sounds good.' They carried on chatting.

They felt comfortable in each other's company.

The next day, she found him in the library as planned, but he had already been there for quite a while. He was making copious notes from a book about the 'Blue Men of the Minch'. This had really caught his attention. He was particularly interested in their description. Apparently, these supposedly mythical creatures inhabited the waters of the Outer Hebrides and the Manes Sea. They were described as being bluish creatures with a humanoid shape. They were agile in the water like dolphins and porpoises, twisting, swimming and diving at great speeds. They were allegedly known to sleep in underwater caves. He was surprised to learn that they also had the power to create fierce storms and that there were many reports of encounters with them.

The librarian called over to her, 'He's been here for hours, do you know him?'

'Oh! he can be a bit intense, but he's okay,' she laughed. But at the same time she thought it was all a bit strange.

As she went over to him, he quickly closed the book he was reading. He didn't want her to ridicule him again. What he had read disturbed him, and he wondered if he had encountered one of these creatures when he had fallen overboard on the day of the storm.

She managed to tear him away from the library.

'Would you like to have a special Grace guide of the island?' she joked.

'Well, if you can find the time for a lonely stranger.' They both laughed. She was pleased to have distracted him.

Over the following days she took him to all the tourist sites. However, he seemed to be most interested in the Emerald Rocks. They were quite spectacular. It was speculated that they had been created by a volcano which had erupted many thousands of years ago. They certainly looked incongruous with their strange jagged edges.

Grace had a thought. 'Would you like to go and have a closer look at the rocks? We can go with my cousin on his boat, he does a tour around the bay. Although he does tend to exaggerate about a strange lobster that he once caught; just take it all with a pinch of salt, he's got a good heart.'

Yan seemed fascinated. 'What do you know about the place?' he asked

'Well, it's quite special, the water seems to turn different colours at certain times of the year.' It's supposed to bring you luck. People often go there to propose or make a wish. My cousin seems to profit from all that stuff,' she laughed.

Yan's face lit up. 'Yes, I would be very interested to do that, but is it safe?' He was still shaken by his recent experiences.

'Oh! don't worry, the boat only goes out when it is calm and I will hold onto you.' At that moment she hugged him, although he seemed to be looking into the distance.

The next day, they boarded *Bob's Tours* and set off into the bay. As they approached the Rocks, Yan had to conceal his feelings of anxiety. There was something about them that disturbed him. He held onto Grace and she felt his unease. However, she was pleased that he was finally becoming more intimate. Then Bob began his monologue about the 'blue lobster' that he had caught after a storm the previous summer; it had been a rare catch and he hadn't stopped boasting about it.

'Yes, I caught a rare blue lobster from here, donated it to science. You know there's only one in a million chance of catching one like that, got a whole article written about me in a science journal, yes they called it Pro -cam -bar us -all -eni.' He stumbled as he spelled out the words.

Yan interrupted him, he was fascinated to learn about it. 'What happened to the specimen?'

'I think it's still living in an aquarium somewhere. I got my picture in the paper and—'

Grace cut in. 'Oh Bobby, you and those flipping stories, you'll be seeing mermaids next!'

He just beamed at her as he revved the boat's engine, which then made a sharp turn, flinging them back against their seats. Yan momentarily felt unnerved and grabbed hold of the side. He was glad that the expedition was over and they were turning back to shore.

Grace felt the next week or so passed far too quickly. Yan was intrigued about the island and continually asked lots of questions. However, he rarely talked about his life in Sweden which concerned Grace, as she would have liked to know more about him.

Grace's mother noticed that she was enamoured with him. 'You seem to be spending a lot of time with that young man, what do you know about him?'

'Stop the inquisition, Mother, it's just a bit of fun!'

'Hmm, is that what you call it? Be careful dear.' She didn't want to pry too much as she hadn't seen Grace be so interested in anyone before.

But the time came when he had to leave. It was all going to end before it had really begun. On the day of his departure they stood together at the quay, pensively looking out across the bay. The call rang out over the Tannoy in the passenger lounge at the ferry terminal.

'This is a call for foot passengers only.' He pulled his backpack onto his shoulders and kissed Grace on the forehead. 'Thanks Grace, I have had such a great time, I hope we can be together again soon.'

'Last call for foot passengers,' rang out again. He gave her one last hug and then he was gone. She felt an aching sadness.

# THE PROPOSAL

A few months passed and she thought that maybe nothing was going to come of it all. She turned over all the things they had said to one another in her mind. She came to the conclusion that maybe he was just a little bit too intense for her, when the phone rang. Her mother answered.

'Grace, there's someone on the phone for you, I can't understand what he is saying.'

She ran down the stairs and nearly fell over. 'Grace is that you?'

'Yes, why?' She didn't want to appear too keen.

'I'm coming back! I've been offered a post, they want me to set up a research station in Port Lar.'

'No, really? Fantastic.' She jumped with excitement.

Yan returned a month later. The idea of a research station in Port lar caused quite a stir, as many of the locals were unsure of the reasons for it. The speculation was that a wind farm was going to be built in the bay and Yan would be doing the survey work. This was certainly not the case but was a useful foil. The area was known for its exceptionally stormy weather and this would have been an ideal location to harness the energy from the wind.

The findings from the equipment that had been salvaged from the research vessel had been analysed at the Science

Institute in Stockholm. They had concluded that some verification was needed about some of the readings. They also wanted further information about the area around the Emerald Rocks. There seemed to be a correlation between some unusual atmospheric disturbances and a strange energy surge emanating from the rocks themselves.

Yan also had two other ulterior motives for returning to Port Lar. The first was to investigate the 'apparition' he had seen that fateful night. He wanted to do further research into reports that had been recorded by local seafarers in the past.

Of course his second motive was to spend more time in Port Lar with Grace.

He took up lodgings in the village in the old house on Briars Hill. It had a panoramic view of the bay. It was an isolated spot, but he thought this was the perfect observation point. He had his telescope trained on the area around the Emerald Rocks. Grace helped him to settle in and visited him almost every day. They seemed to be in each other's company constantly. She would often accompany him in the motor cruiser around the bay, while he set and adjusted various pieces of equipment.

Grace was intrigued by him. She wasn't sure why. She wondered if it was because he was just so different from all the men she had known. He could be charming and affectionate, but also distant. She wasn't sure if this was a cultural thing or his particular type of personality. She did worry about his shifting moods and the fact that he could be incomprehensible at times. He became particularly moody when they discussed the subject of the underwater creature he had seen on the night of the storm. Grace, however, had her own plausible explanation which irritated him.

'You know you did have a nasty gash on your head that night, when you went overboard ...'

'So, you think I made it up? Well I think you could try to open your mind a little more,' he replied angrily.

She felt disconcerted by his sharpness and thought he was being unduly hard on her as she only wanted to allay his fears. Then he smiled at her and she assumed he was just making fun of her. It was obvious that they were becoming more than fond of each other. He was bright, witty and extremely knowledgeable about all sorts of things. She was fascinated by him. He felt very comfortable with her. They would spend hours on the cliffs looking down towards the bay.

Yan was driven by a fascination for the Emerald Rocks and began to intensively study their incongruous nature. He was torn between scientific facts, local knowledge and legends. He had discovered that the blue glow which emanated around them was not just attributed to the reflection of the sun but also from something much more mysterious. He couldn't quite reconcile the science. The local legends, he felt, were becoming oddly more convincing. He wondered if there really was something supernatural about them.

Yan and Grace made several further trips around them. On one of these trips Grace noticed Yan looking different. He had an unusual expression on his face.

'Are you okay?' she asked.

'Yes, yes I think we should get off at the landing stage.' He looked sheepish

They alighted from their boat and wandered across the

stony beach to an observation hut.

Yan then pushed the door open. There was a small table lit with candles, a bottle of wine and two glasses.

'Wow, what's going on here?' said Grace

Yan stood by the table and beckoned her to sit down, he looked on edge and was perspiring.

'I need to ask you something.'

Grace fell silent, this was all very out of character.

'Yes, what?' She replied hesitantly.

'Grace, since I met you I have felt ...' he paused and then he looked strangely vulnerable. He took a deep breath and quietly said, 'I, I think, I, well I'm quite certain that I most definitely love you!' 'Really?' She looked at him. There was a silence, he looked awkward.

'Do you think you could possibly entertain the idea of marrying me?'

For a moment she looked stunned. It was all very sudden, but somehow exciting, nothing like this had ever happened to her before. She blushed.

'Yes, I ... well, what the hell?' she thought for a moment.

'Yes let's do it.' This was impulsive and exciting, she jumped with excitement and shouted on the top of her voice, 'I will marry you, Yan Ericson, absolutely of course!' She nervously laughed, as he passed her a glass of wine and kissed her.

Then Yan continued, 'We must do it straight away!' He looked intense, it was as if he knew this was something he had to do quickly.

'Okay, yes, why not?' She had always wanted to do things differently.

There was something inevitable about it.

The nuptials were arranged very quickly. Her mother was concerned about the haste. She thought it was a whirlwind romance and tried to talk some sense into Grace.

'Oh Grace, I am so happy for you, but why the rush?' Although she knew her somewhat headstrong daughter was not going to listen to her.

'We just want to have a small reception, no fuss!'

So a small reception was arranged with Grace's family and a few friends. There would only be a couple of Yan's friends from Sweden and he wasn't sure if they would be able to make it. Yan had no close family as his parents had died quite tragically when he was a small child, leaving him to be brought up by his grandmother. Unfortunately, she was now too infirm to travel.

Grace asked her uncle to give her away. He was happy to oblige as Grace was his favourite niece. However, there was something about Yan that disturbed him. He felt that he was cold and distant and he worried that Grace had been too eager to embark on marriage without knowing more about him.

The day of the wedding was a fairly quiet affair. They were married in a small Methodist chapel that was located on the cliff top. It was a simple ceremony. Grace looked serene and vulnerable in her bridal attire. As she took her uncle's arm to make her entrance into the chapel, he felt unsure and anxious about the whole thing and whispered in her ear, 'Grace, you know you can change your mind: you don't have to marry him just yet.'

She thought this was an odd thing to say at that particular moment. Although she too had a feeling of hesitation, she put it all down to nerves. It wouldn't be easy for Yan to gain acceptance. The islanders were wary of strangers. Yan's mannerisms would definitely be construed as odd. She also had to concede she really didn't really know a lot about him. However, it was that mystery that had drawn her to him in the first place.

The day seemed to pass very quickly. However, for Yan, it was the first time in a long time that he felt happy. Sadly for much of his youth, he had ached with loneliness. His grandmother had tried her best to raise him but he felt he had missed out by not having a real family. Now that he had Grace, he began to feel more complete. For Grace it had all been a bit of a whirlwind. Yan was unlike anyone she had known.

They decided that they would continue to live at the old house on the top of the cliff. The old house was a bit desolate but Yan had grown very fond of it. He continued to conduct his research. Grace completed her course at the college and managed to get a permanent job at the garden centre. Everything seemed to be going well, then Grace fell pregnant.

Grace's mother, however, felt a little concerned.

'You know, Grace, we hardly see you, you don't seem to come down into the village very often. I'm worried about you.'

'Stop worrying, things are just busy at the moment with Yan's research and work.'

'When the baby arrives, I can always help out.'

'Thanks Mum, but Yan wants me to quit my job and look after the baby myself.'

Her mum looked slightly perturbed. 'But you are going

to get very lonely up there on your own, Yan seems to be out on the boat all the time, you are going to need some time to yourself. I can—'

Grace butted in, 'Stop Mum, you are just interfering. We are fine, honest.'

Her mother realised she wasn't really listening. She thought that they were becoming too isolated from everyone. She wasn't sure about Yan either; of late he had become too controlling of Grace.

In no time at all the baby was born. It was a boy they called Ben. His birth seemed to brighten Yan, and he became a devoted father. For a while everything seemed perfect, although something seemed to be disturbing him.

Grace noticed Yan wasn't sleeping properly and seemed quite agitated.

He would mutter to himself and call out in a strange language. She thought maybe it was Swedish but she couldn't identify any of the words. He also began to sleepwalk and she would often find him in the morning in the study, hunched over his desk asleep. She thought it was just the stress of running the project and having a new family, although she noticed he had become more and more irritable, particularly when it was stormy. The winter months could be particularly wild and he seemed to get more agitated. On one such bleak evening she heard him call up to her while she was upstairs.

'Grace, just going to take the readings.'

'Okay, but don't be long, it's wild out there and Ben's taking ages to settle down.'

'When I come back I will sit with him.'

Yan wanted to help as much as possible. However,

he was working tirelessly on the project. It had become evident to him that the seismic activity was the result of something far from normal. His suspicions were just about to be confirmed, and he was on the verge of an incredible discovery. It dawned on him that he needed to document his evidence and hide it. His analysis was that there was something beyond the 'norm' occurring. He was unaware that his behaviour was changing quite dramatically. He was more intense and more preoccupied by his work, spending longer and longer periods at the Emerald Rocks.

His initial research highlighted some strange occurrences in their geology. The haphazard readings also indicated strange seismic activity in the bay itself. He was also investigating the very peculiar way in which organisms had attached themselves to the rocks. This was both perplexing and incongruous to his scientific mind and most definitely pointed towards something scientifically controversial.

He became increasingly aware that there was something extraordinarily mysterious about the Emerald Rocks, and couldn't quite understand the feeling that something seemed to be attracting him towards them. He continued with his work as best he could although something seemed to be dictating his every move. On this particularly stormy night the feeling had become so intense that he felt compelled to go out and inspect the instruments in the bay.

Grace called him again, 'Take care.' She felt a sudden panic, and thought it was odd that he had to do this. It was getting late.

He had then quietly slipped out. She remembered

hearing him open the latch on the back door. Ben seemed to take an age to settle and she had fallen asleep with him tucked under her shoulder. When she woke up, she glanced at her watch. It was nearly 11 o'clock and Yan had not returned. She called her uncle at the pub, although he said he had not seen him. He asked various clientele in the pub, 'Anyone seen Yan? Gracie says he's not gone home.'

'I saw him wandering along the pier. Surprised he went down there with the waves being so huge,' replied old Geoff, who had been in the vicinity walking his dog.

'It seems a bit odd, it's very late,' thought George.

'Might be a good idea to tell the coastguard.'

As the weather had deteriorated, a search was made but by the next day it had become all too apparent that he was missing. During the following weeks the grim realisation began to sink in. Yan had somehow drowned, although his body was never found. Graces' life was turned upside down. In her heart of hearts she knew he was gone but she couldn't accept it. She felt a desperate longing, a void that could not be filled. The only compensation was Ben. It would have been hard to cope without him.

# BEN

The years drifted by. Grace was left to raise Ben as best she could. Friends and family tried to help her through the grief, but Ben was the only real consolation for the heartbreak. His friendly, playful character was a distraction from loneliness and despair. He was now approaching sixteen and it was hard for her to believe that he had grown up so quickly. She was sometimes unnerved by his similarity to his father. He had grown quite tall and had the same blue eyes and straight blonde hair. His fringe, which he was constantly fiddling with, hung untidily across his eyes. He was very bright and inquisitive.

Today was an important day for Ben as he was taking the last of his exams. She stood at the bottom of the stairs and called to him, 'Hurry up, you will miss your bus!'

Ben was taking his time as usual. He had done as much revision as he could and now longed to be free from the constraints of school. He pensively looked out of the window across the bay. He grabbed his school bag and headed to the landing at the top of the stairs. He rested his head on his hand and stared at the painting on the wall. It had always captured his attention and somehow disturbed him. The scruffy canvas seemed to possess a strange allure. There was something about the scene it depicted and its intricate detail which mesmerised him. He did not hear his mother's voice, then she shouted again

'Five minutes. Come on you will be late again for school!'

He continued to ignore her. A hand landed on his shoulder, a soft voice echoed in his ears.

'Your father painted that.'

She took in a deep breath and held back a tear.

The painting had hung there ever since he could remember. Grace had not been able to take it down. It depicted a cityscape, with strange futuristic architecture. The buildings seemed to have an organic quality, and were painted in strange muted colours. There were many different elevations. He was drawn to what seemed to be a complex of spherical structures dominating the skyline. He wondered what its purpose was. However, the most intriguing aspect was a vast translucent dome which seemed to envelop the city itself. He was transfixed by it and tried to imagine the inhabitants.

'Come on, Ben, time to go.'

Grace adjusted his shirt collar, which exposed a hastily tied tie. She turned him in the direction of the front door.

'Good luck with the exam, you will be fine. Your father would have been so proud of you.' She waved him off, with a cheerful smile, hiding the depth of grief that every thought of Yan brought.

Ben ambled along the winding road to the bus stop. On the way he removed his tie and shoved it into the side pocket of his backpack, where it carelessly dangled.

As he ventured along the road, each twist and turn seemed to hold strong memories. He began to have a strong sense of deja vu. This was a well-trodden path of wild imaginings and childhood adventures. He smiled to himself as he passed the crumbling wall by farmer Jessop's barn. He remembered imagining himself as a gladiator and the many duels he had had with an imaginary black knight. He had also outwitted 'The Raven king', (a somewhat shabby looking rook that happened to land on farmer Blythe's fence) and he'd outrun 'Sam', the evil one eyed ram who had stalked him from behind the black sheds.

He sighed and now realised that this had all been so temporary, merely a rite of passage. Those distant battles were just memories: the wall looked quite ordinary now, the fence was broken and the barn had fallen into disrepair. His thoughts were now so very different, so much more complex. He was now driven by something more. He leaned against the side of the bus shelter and spied the school bus edging its way along the road. This would be the last journey into school before the summer holidays. He didn't have to wait for long, as the bus arrived within minutes. He got on and ignored the rabble that were about to unleash their well-practised bravado. In unison they shouted out, 'Wanker wanker you're a plonker.'

They thought this was hilarious. They jumped up and down on the back seat and squashed their faces against the window, which seemed to make them contorted and more menacing. He ignored them, and found his way to an unoccupied seat. Their attention soon shifted to another target; an unsuspecting driver in the car behind the bus. They started flashing V signs. The driver accelerated and overtook the bus, shaking his head in disgust.

The bus driver glared and shouted at the rowdy kids in

the back seat, 'If you don't pack it in I'm gonna throw you off the bus!'

As the bus continued along the road, Ben sank into his seat, pulled his hoodie over his face and stared out of the window.

The image of the painting seemed to fill his thoughts and he felt himself being transported into its landscape.

'It is possible. Anything is possible in an infinite universe,' he said to himself.

Then the bus stopped and unburdened its rowdy load onto the playground. The driver, momentarily relieved of this burden, sighed with relief and continued on to his next destination.

Ben followed the noisy rabble into the school. He headed towards the library and found a quiet corner where he could gather his thoughts. The pressure was on him to do well and he didn't want to let his mother down. He opened his bag and got out his text book. He tapped the table with his pencil.

At that moment Mr Bates, his science teacher, spied him through the library door window and waved to catch his attention. Mr Bates had the nickname of 'Batty Bates' as he was a somewhat eccentric character. He had a hearing problem for which he was mercilessly teased by some of the less desirable pupils. He also had a strong Welsh accent which became incomprehensible when he was angry.

'Ah mathematics today, Ben, well done, good luck, can see you tapping the old pencil there. How are you feeling – not too nervous?'

'Am fine, sir. Actually I was just wondering about other things – bigger things.'

'Ah yes life is a wonder, boy! Who knows what life is all about eh? Does it really matter, when you really think about it? We might all yet be annihilated at any moment!'

Ben liked Mr Bates, he was open minded with a tendency to exaggerate, and was convinced that humanity was doomed.

'Do you really think that, sir?' replied Ben, who was trying to smile and be polite.

'Yes, not a theory, a distinct possibility! Just think in a parallel universe there could be an exact copy of a boy like you but for one tiny detail!'

He looked at his watch and realised he was late for his next class.

'Unfortunately, at this moment in time in this particular universe there's the horrible squirmy little buggers of Nine B, just too much to conjecture, boy. Anyway, I must get on, good luck, talk to you later.'

As he turned to leave he gently pulled the tie from Ben's backpack and gestured for him to put it on. Ben reluctantly put it on. He didn't want to attract any more attention today.

For 'Batty Bates', the prospect of 9B's company for the next hour was enough for him to hope the world would soon end. He continued down the corridor, and as he reached the classroom door, he ducked under the window and listened. As usual a trap was being set for him. He overheard their shouts.

'Quick, it's Batty Bates, get back to your seat!'

He slammed the door open with such force that a row of books fell off the shelf behind it.

With deft accuracy he picked up a board rubber from

his desk and slung it at the back wall, from which it then rebounded and skimmed the ear of a weasel-faced boy nicknamed 'Tooley' who was sniggering to his mate.

'Ouch!' shouted Tooley who rubbed his ear.

There was a gasp from the class. Tooley's eyes narrowed, there was a pregnant pause.

He would not be outdone by this manoeuvre from Batty Bates!

A flash of ingenuity crossed his meagre brain. He began to mime a long sentence, while staring directly at Mr Bates.

Mr Bates began to furiously fiddle with his hearing aid and swore under his breath.

'Oh bugger. What are you saying you little cretin?'

Uproar and riotous laughter ensued as the classroom descended into chaos.

Mr Bates tried to control the ruckus, but to no avail. His credibility had faded. Tooley basked in the adulation of the class and smiled as his teacher floundered.

Ben could hear the commotion which was going on as he passed by 9B. He felt sorry for poor old Bates. They had spent much time together discussing the complexities of human evolution and the possible parallel existence of other worlds. Mr Bates had introduced him to all manner of fascinating theories. It was sad that a teacher as interesting as him was currently enduring such humiliation.

Ben then made his way to the assembly hall where neat rows of tables greeted him. He found his place, and the invigilator handed out the papers. He arranged his writing implements neatly on the desk then stared down at the questions and waited.

A voice echoed around the hall, as the second hand on

the clock reached the hour. He heard, 'You may begin,' and set to work.

He picked up his pen, the next three hours seemed to pass in an instant. At the end of the exam he stared ahead exhausted. He flexed and stretched his fingers and sighed with relief, knowing that finally it was all over.

As he left the hall, he noticed that Mr Bates was standing in the corridor by the main noticeboard in discussion with the head. The head was a man of quite short stature. He always wore impeccable suits and had highly polished shoes. He had mastered the art of shining each shoe on the back of the opposite trouser leg while maintaining an upright position standing on one leg. His hair was short and severely cut. When he was feeling irritated he would twitch his face slightly and curl up his bottom lip. The more agitated he became, the more his piggy little eyes would narrow and sink into his chubby, masklike face.

Ben heard him respond to Batesy's futile remonstrations with his well-practised staccato.

'Mr Bates, we must be confident that the pupil's welfare is not compromised.'

To which Batesy replied, 'Those boys need discipline, headmaster, discipline!'

He was red in the face and perspiring heavily.

'Monday, meeting with Mr Toole, don't be late.'

The head glared at him. Mr Bates looked positively distraught. As he cast his eyes around he saw Ben ambling along the corridor and seized the moment.

'Excuse me, headmaster, I must have a chat with young Ben there.' He turned and swiftly caught up with Ben.

'Ericson, Ben my boy, wait a moment.'

The head looked exasperated

'Don't forget the meeting, Mr Bates,' he barked.

But Mr Bates had vanished, the head just sighed. He knew it would be difficult to change the controversial teaching methods of his colleague. He turned his attention to a group of boys who were huddled in a corner and reprimanded them for being late for class.

Mr Bates, however, had made his escape and fixed his attention on Ben.

'Ah Ben, yes, we said we'd have a talk. First of all, how did it go?'

Ben could see that Batesy had had a run in with the head, and it felt wrong that he was being maligned in such an undignified way. He smiled and replied, 'I think it went well, at least I answered all the questions.'

'Yes, life is one big question my boy. Perhaps there is one universal question?'

'If a question makes you think then it's worth asking,' replied Ben.

Mr Bates was pleased with his reply and smiled.

'Yes you certainly have more insight in your little finger than some I could mention. Anyway, did you read that chapter on dimensional manipulation? The Merkabah Vehicle, very interesting. The possibility of travelling to higher dimensional planes and transcending the physical body altogether?'

Ben wasn't really sure what Batesy was talking about. He seemed to be rambling into areas that confused him.

'I've got to go now, sir.'

Then he ran off to join his friend Robbie, who was waiting for him by the school lockers.

'Yes, quite, another time perhaps? Enjoy the summer vacation!'

Mr Bates wandered back along the corridor lost in his thoughts about higher dimensional travel. When he reached the staff room Mr Briggs the PE teacher accosted him and teasingly gloated.

'I believe you've got an interesting interview with Mr Toole!' Mr Bates ignored him and silently collected some books from his cubby hole.

The school bell tolled jarringly, signalling the end of the school day and, greatly relieved, he stepped into the corridor and was carried along with the swell of pupils who were equally eager to escape.

# THE PARENTS MEETING

Over the years Mr Bates had become a lonely eccentric. His theorising tended to provide people with a little momentary amusement, but his constant preoccupation with them had become irritating for most. He was deeply obsessed with all kinds of theories concerning the cosmos. Astronomy was a passion and he would spend many an evening staring through his telescope, transfixed by the night sky. The slightest irregularity in star patterns had him trembling with excitement. Unfortunately, few people appreciated either his enthusiasm or his constant revelations. Most people would invent any excuse to distance themselves from his verbal rambles and wild staring eyes. He did not endear himself to his colleagues for many reasons. He also had a pronounced body odour problem, exacerbated by his habit of spraying deodorant on the outside of his shirts. It was inevitable that he was an easy target for unkind remarks.

If it wasn't for the fact that one or two of the more tolerant teachers were quite amiable with him, his life would have been unbearable.

Mr White, the new social sciences teacher, did at least pass the time of day with him. He didn't have the heart to ignore him. However, this did on occasion lead to a few awkward moments. He was sitting in the staff room one day marking when Mr Bates sidled up to him. Mr Bates fixed his eyes firmly on him and stared for a moment, then there was a moment of silence.

'The question is, Mr White, why did the oscillation of Opus Two affect its moon's trajectory?'

'Sorry, I didn't quite catch that,' replied Mr White who was hastily trying to mark a set of exam papers. 'Was it on one of the science papers?'

He had presumed Mr Bates was also marking and was puzzled by the fact that the question was in fact drawn purely from thin air.

Of course Mr Bates hadn't even started his marking, he had been far too preoccupied.

Mr White was the head's new 'golden boy'. The head referred to him as 'JW'. In his mind he felt it made him seem like he was 'getting down' with the younger staff, which he most definitely wasn't. The nickname, however, had stuck and everyone referred to him as JW, apart from Mr Bates.

JW was blessed with both looks and intelligence. He was quite tall, and sported a head of blonde tousled locks which were rarely combed, lending him a somewhat boyish appeal. The female staff admired him and he was also liked by the pupils.

The head had decided to delegate to him the somewhat tricky interview between Mr Toole and Mr Bates. This was another opportunity for JW to prove his worth.

Mr Toole senior was not an easy character to deal with. He was a thick-set, thuggish looking man. He owned a ramshackle farm on the edge of Port Lar, which looked almost derelict. It had once been quite idyllic, but after his wife had died things had taken a turn for the worse. The old barns were falling to pieces, their rusty corrugated roofs were now in a dilapidated state. They had taken a beating during last winter's storms and twisted sheets of rusty steel hung dangerously from their weakened trusses.

Mr Tool hoarded all manner of mechanical hardware. One of the more unusual items was an old Second World War tank. It was carefully hidden away beneath some cargo netting as there had recently been something of an 'incident'. He had had a 'bit of a do' one night after a very heavy drinking session and for reasons best known to himself had gone berserk.

For some reason, he had climbed into the tank and driven it the wrong way down the promenade. He had gone through the railings and over the wall, and ended up on the beach. In the process he had demolished a couple of lampposts and a telephone box. As he drove along the beach the tide had begun to come in and he had been marooned. Word got out that he was 'off his head' and young Tooley promptly went to his rescue.

If it had not been for his son he might have drowned. At the tender age of fifteen, young Tooley had learned to drive most of the vehicles on the farm. He had raced along the twisty roads in a tractor at top speed and managed to reverse down the lifeboat slipway to where the tank was slowly sinking into the sand. Fortunately, he managed to tow him back out of danger.

It was a struggle for Mr Toole senior to bring up his one and only son 'Tooley', who was now a law unto himself. He had run wild. He was as unkempt as his father and had a fearsome reputation amongst the children of the school. Mr Toole, however, would not have a word said against his son, particularly after proving his worth in this recent rescue of the tank.

An official letter from the headmaster had been sent to Mr Toole about his son's behaviour, which had put him in a foul mood. He had been asked to attend a parental meeting which he had tried to wriggle out of. However, after telephoning the school, the school secretary in her own indomitable fashion put him in his place.

'Now, Mr Toole you have an obligation to attend this meeting, otherwise we will have to pass this on to social services.'

He berated her in his usual fashion, 'Don't you F ... ing tell me what to do!'

She crisply replied, 'Nine am, Monday, don't be late!'

So, now it was up to JW to sort it all out and make sure no blood was spilled.

That following Monday JW bumped into Mr Bates as he was standing by the pigeon holes in the staffroom.

'Ah, Mr Bates there you are,' he smiled. 'Isn't young Ben Ericson in one of your classes?'

'Yes, bright lad,' replied Mr Bates.

'Do you think he will get an 'A' in science?'

'Oh yes yes, shows a lot of promise, yes.'

He was keen to show off their good relationship.

'Hmm, do you not think he has a tendency to be a little overimaginative?'

'No, no no no, quite the opposite, very pragmatic.'

He was quite taken aback by Mr White's criticism of his best pupil.

'Yup, maybe, maybe, blasted reports, maths teacher says he's always banging on about wormholes and black holes and the like!'

'Is he, is he?'

Batesy looked slightly abashed.

'Anyway, about Mr Toole.'

'Mr Toole?' replied Mr Bates

JW had to think quickly, Mr Bates had forgotten all about Mr Toole. 'Now, shall we just go over one or two points before the meeting.' JW looked concerned.

'Could I just share something I have been deliberating about?' replied Batesy.

'Sure. What's the problem?'

JW put his hands in his pockets and fiddled with some coins.

'It's about, well, a kind of discovery. Something really fascinating, extraordinary.'

'Right, first things first, about this meeting?'

JW tried to keep him on the task, but Mr Bates wasn't listening and seemed unaware of his possible fate at the hands of Mr Toole.

Batesy continued, 'You see I think I may have stumbled upon—'

JW cut in again, 'Perhaps you shouldn't mention calling him a cretin. Let me do the talking eh!'

'Of course there's every possibility that—'

Batesy was all fired up and staring wildly. JW was exasperated and interrupted again. 'Look at the time, we are already late, we need to get going, can't keep Mr Toole waiting! Just leave all the talking to me,' said JW, gesturing to him to sit outside the office.

Mr Bates continued to fiddle with some papers, and mumbled to himself.

JW led Batesy into the interview room. They sat down uncomfortably behind a table. JW began to shuffle various papers. Mr Bates sat nervously twisting his hands. The room was quite small and stuffy. JW got up and attempted to open a window, but there was a wind blowing outside which sent a draft across the table, blowing the neat pile of papers everywhere. At that moment the secretary appeared with Mr Toole.

'Ah, here we are Mr Toole.' She left him standing there staring at Mr Bates.

'Oops, sorry, the wind.' JW frantically picked up the papers and returned to his seat trying not to look ruffled.

He tried to put on a friendly face. 'Ah nice to see you, Mr Toole, shall we get on?'

Mr Toole pointed at Mr Bates and snarled, 'I want him sacked!'

'Now, now let's see if we can just talk about this shall we?' said JW.

Mr Bates was both agitated and distracted. Even during this exchange he was actually completely preoccupied with higher matters. He interjected the occasional 'Yes' and 'No' to the conversation but was obviously in another mental space altogether. He was sweating profusely and constantly fidgeting. Something clearly had unnerved him, but it had nothing to do with Mr Toole. Indeed, he seemed to be completely oblivious to the threats and accusations that were being hurled at him.

'If he picks on me lad one more time I'm gonna kill him!' snorted Mr Toole.

'Now, now we wouldn't want to be doing that.'

JW did his best to console him. Eventually, after many mumblings and distracted apologies on Mr Bates behalf, he managed to calm him down. Mr Toole left the meeting red in the face and wanting the last word, snarling 'Gawd! he stinks wuss than me pigs!'

# THE DISCOVERY

The previous Friday night, Mr Bates had been invited to attend the opening of an exhibition at the local museum. Mr Bates had drawn the short straw of the school staff, as no one else wanted to be involved in such an obscure and stuffy occasion. He had arrived early, which was unusual for him because generally he was always late.

He was met by Miss Pringle, the head librarian. Miss Pringle was a woman who tended to fuss. She was eager for the evening to go well and was busy repositioning the chairs as he walked into the room.

She was a somewhat rotund woman, with slight little features. It was almost as though her face hadn't quite developed.

'Oh wonderful, glad you could make it, Mr Bates isn't it?'

'Yes, yes.'

As he didn't want to hang around chatting to her, he excused himself rapidly.

'Excuse me I just need to freshen up.'

'Of course, of course, down the corridor on the right, next to the storeroom.'

She stood back a little, perplexed by his brusqueness. The flower arrangement suddenly demanded her complete attention.

As Mr Bates wandered down the corridor he noticed that the storeroom door was open. This seemed a good place to take solace for a while and compose himself before the dreaded presentations.

The storeroom shelves were untidily stuffed with all sorts of artefacts, books and documents. He found himself intrigued by an old brown cardboard box which was dangling precariously from a back shelf. He tried to push it to one side but as he did, it fell apart and the contents tumbled onto the floor. As he tried to pick up the contents his attention was caught by some papers tied with a piece of string. He muttered under his breath.

'What on earth can these be?' Then he was suddenly taken aback. A familiar name was inscribed on one of the folders. He read it out loud.

'Yan Ericson, Operation Emerald. Hmm how very interesting! It must be a bit of his oceanic research.'

After studying the outer cover, his curiosity got the better of him.

'Perhaps a quick look,' he muttered and turned the first page. To his astonishment the title read 'PLANET X', which very much caught his attention.

He felt compelled to flick through its mottled and dingy pages. The information was almost unreadable. However, he was fascinated.

He then read the words, 'The Triangulum Galaxy, three billion light years from Earth, nineth planet of the red sun, hmm very interesting!'

He saw that there were several star maps.

'Ah, oh my goodness!'

His eyes widened and he scratched his head.

The text had suffered from age and neglect but another phrase caught his eye.

'Two moons!' he caught his breath. 'This is most unusual.' Then he remembered about the presentation.

'Damn that woman, no time to look at it now, I'll read it later.'

He knew Miss Pringle would be looking for him. As he stood contemplating his discovery he could hear the progressively louder clip clopping of Miss Pringle's heels and then her rather breathless voice shouting.

'Mr Bates, Mr Bates are you there? We are waiting for you.'

She was clearly agitated. Before he could turn around she was standing at the door.

'Ah, I see you are looking at those old files.'

'Yes, do you know anything about them?'

'Yes, I think there was a foreign chap, you know the one who was tragically drowned years ago? Terrible, terrible for that poor young woman. Are you interested in them?'

'I know his son, Ben, do you think I could borrow them?'

'Of course, they are just gathering dust here. I was going to dispose of it all next week.' She grabbed his arm, which made him feel uncomfortable, and said brightly,

'We must get on, Mr Bates, on to the opening!' and ushered him back to the exhibition.

He stuffed the file into his bag, pondering on how it was that Ben's father had come into possession of such intriguing facts. He knew that Ben's father had been involved in some kind of 'scientific outreach' survey work in the area. This had involved collecting data from various instruments which were located at strategic points around the bay. His activity at the time had drawn all sorts of speculation from the locals. Most were convinced that he was working for a renewable energy company who planned to install wind turbines offshore. However, this was not the case, as he was in fact working on a very obscure research project. His task was to confirm some highly unusual scientific data that had been collected in the area.

The material that Mr Bates had discovered referred to some of these extraordinary facts. It seemed that Yan Ericson had compounded evidence of incidents that could only be explained in terms of an interaction with an alternative dimension. He had documented precise coordinates, dates and times going back through several centuries. The evidence was conclusive.

For Mr Bates, to finally possess evidence of his wildest hypotheses was more than he could ever have imagined. He could hardly contain himself. He felt a sense of profound inner satisfaction, as his theories were at last vindicated by what seemed to be hard scientific facts. Given its shattering importance, he could not understand how this material could have been abandoned. He shrugged off his feelings of hesitation and tried to justify keeping the information to himself, muttering under his breath, 'I wonder if Ben's father must have simply mislaid it, yes, yes that's what he has done!'

That thought seemed to give him permission to hold onto his incredible find at least until his curiosity was sated.

Throughout the evening he was completely preoccupied and hardly able to contain himself. He just about managed to bumble his way through the presentation.

All he wanted to do was to return home. He wasn't good at public occasions and the thought of having to speak in front of a dreary set of dignitaries from the local council was exhausting. He took his leave at the earliest opportunity.

He lived in a grimy little apartment, which was on the ground floor of a Victorian house which had seen better days. The landlord had not kept the property in good condition. However, it suited Mr Bates as the rent was cheap. He climbed the once elegant steps to the front door and was greeted by a startled pigeon, which flapped in his face and deposited further excrement on the already heavily encrusted stonework. He fumbled for the key and pushed open the door that seemed to lead to a distinctive hallway reminiscent of Victorian splendour and of days gone by. He shuffled along the passageway to his apartment.

Once inside, he bolted the door and fastened the key chain. He had endured some unpleasant intrusions in the past and needed to feel secure. He then went to draw the curtains in the sitting room. The illumination from the outside street lamps cast a dismal shadow, adding to the overall grubbiness of the place.

He retired to the living room. There was a half-filled bottle of Scotch on the mantelpiece. He filled a murky looking glass with the amber liquid, and plonked himself down on an old tatty leather armchair. The coffee table was covered in newspapers, books and detritus, which had been gathering dust. He clumsily cleared a space and then retrieved the folder from his briefcase. He stared at it for a few moments and then opened it.

He was immediately transfixed. He began muttering to himself, 'What's this? This is impossible, my God, how on earth, oh dieu, dieu.'

There were references and extracts from books about myths and legends. He flicked through some of the annotated pages.

'Extraordinary, what was he looking for? This is very odd, very odd, the Blue Man? What's this? Strange activities in the sea, from another world?'

He was intrigued and began to scan the pages as fast as could.

'My goodness, what a revelation,' he sighed. 'Ah yes, creatures living in deep underwater caves. The "Emerald Rocks" oh my word, interesting, of all places! Dieu dieu, this is remarkable, truly remarkable!'

He skimmed through several pages of astronomical charts, which had some strange geometrical patterns and symbols. A red marker outlined what seemed to be the coordinates of a planet from far beyond our solar system. It had been given the name 'Planet X'.

Although intoxicated by these discoveries, he began to experience a heady feeling of exhaustion. He wasn't sure what he would do with all this material. He thought about Ben, and struggled with his conscience.

'I must pass this on to young Ben, yes that's what I should do, yes, yes, I'll post it to him. We can discuss it together, yes, that's what his father would have wanted, yes.'

He was at odds with himself. His thoughts drifted. He thought about all the great scientists and their aspirations. He remembered the prophetic words of Carl Sagan,

*'We find that we live on an insignificant planet, a*

*humdrum star lost in a galaxy tucked away in some forgotten corner of a universe in which there are far more galaxies than people.'*

These words hung on the wall of the science department in Ben's school. It was his favourite quote. He was in awe of physicists and cosmologists who had for many years deliberated on the possibility of other alien worlds.

He could hardly believe that he had inadvertently stumbled onto something relating to the existence of life on a distant planet. There was more to this than he could ever have imagined.

He drifted off and slept uncomfortably in the armchair. He dreamed of far flung galaxies and wondrous places. He could not have foreseen the events that were about to unfold in this sleepy remote island in the middle of the Manes Sea.

# THE ENTANGLEMENT

The search and rescue teams who scoured the bay for several days after Yan's disappearance found no indications as to what had happened. It was generally agreed that it was unusual that his body had not washed ashore. Without a body the coroner was unable to close the case, and so for all intents and purposes Yan was legally a missing person.

Although Mr Bates now had information which could point towards what may have happened on the night of Yan's disappearance, it was doubtful if anyone would believe him. He was now completely convinced that Yan's disappearance was connected to an interaction of alien origin.

The revolutionary nature of Yan's investigations had in fact drawn the attention of various government agencies. As they were concerned about issues of national security, the university had been obliged to keep them informed of his progress. Unknown to anyone at this point, something not of this world was indeed at the heart of his investigations. Quite by chance he had discovered a unique phenomenon beneath the Manes Sea. It was then that his fate was sealed.

His first encounter with the inexplicable occurred when he was swept overboard during the storm. When he fell into the water he came face to face with a presence he subsequently referred to as the 'Blue Man'. He knew he had encountered something beyond human experience but he had no inkling of its meaning.

On the night of his disappearance, the instruments that he had set on the Emerald Rocks had displayed highly unusual seismic and electrical activity. He knew he had to check its veracity. By checking manually he thought he might finally be able to understand the nature of the energy surges. As he left the comfort of his home, he buttoned his jacket and pulled his hood over his head. If things went well it would only take about an hour to get the job done. For some reason he glanced back wistfully towards the house and thought of Ben and Grace. As he wandered along the quay and looked out towards the Emerald Rocks he was strangely anxious, and more than that, he remembered that it was the same feeling as when he was thrown overboard on the night of the storm. As he steered his boat towards the Emerald Rocks he began to feel dizzy and faint. His vision blurred, and as a dark dizziness overcame him he lost consciousness. After an unknown time, he came to, and found himself swirling inside some kind of vortex. His physical body seemed absent. He was floating and drifting, weightless and in darkness. He became nauseous and deeply afraid. Then he heard a voice.

'Do not be alarmed, we are not going to harm you,' the voice seemed to register in his mind, yet was not audible.

'Where am I? What's happening to me?' he voiced, again without seeming to make any sound.

'We are trying to connect the temporal lobes,' a voice droned in a monotone. As he attempted to collect his wits he felt completely disorientated. He seemed to be lying on some kind of platform that was floating in mid-air. There were beings standing over him which, although they were humanoid in shape, were not human. A bluish light seemed to emanate from them. He was aware of himself as a being, but not as a body. He called out, although, as in a dream, there was no sound.

He called out again. 'Where am I? Who are you? What do you want with me?' he pleaded.

It was then that he became aware that there was something familiar about this encounter. He knew he had felt like this once before. He cried again, 'Where am I?' and as he gazed up at the shapes of the beings around him, he felt a sudden jolt of recognition. As much to himself as to them, he muttered the words, 'Are you the Blue Men?'

'The Blue Men, what does he mean?' The creatures surrounding him made adjustments to an array of instruments on a panel beside him. An image appeared on a monitor above him, which exactly displayed his encounter with the presence he had encountered in the water when he had been thrown overboard in the storm. A voice addressed him again.

'For some time we have been excavating in this zone via means that you would not understand. You encountered this activity and your mind invented the creature that you have called the Blue Man. It is unfortunate that we have disturbed your species. This was never our intention.'

'What do you want with me?'

'You have knowledge of great significance to us.'

Yan stumbled in his thoughts. 'You are real. Who are you?'

'Do not be alarmed.' There was a pause, and in the

silence he felt his mind go blank, and then it began to fill with images beyond his comprehension.

He could hear voices but they were not addressed to him. They were full of concern and there seemed to be considerable disagreement as to what should be done. Amongst all the discussion he repeatedly heard them say, 'The programme has been compromised.' He also heard some discussion about the probe being realigned and something about the need to keep the subject alive until then.

Yan had been of interest to these creatures for some time. After his encounter with the strange watery entity during the night of the storm, a connection had been made. As time passed after the encounter he began to have more experiences just beyond the realm of normal thought and often had disturbing dreams. He wondered if it was something simply in the legends of the 'Blue Man' that was disturbing his subconscious. However, the entity he had thought was the 'Blue Man' was no legend.

Visions of a distant planet disturbed his sleep at first, but then began to manifest even when he was awake. During these times he had also experienced some kind of presence. He could not have known the reality of his situation. He did not know that he was being observed and manipulated. As these experiences grew in intensity the 'presence' acted decisively. It was decided that he could not remain on Earth. There were complex reasons for his abduction, involving the fate of an entire civilisation.

His 'extraction' was not altogether successful. The method and speed in which it was expedited was somewhat careless. Not enough time was taken to ensure that all the safety precautions necessary to ensure a human's survival were put into place. The device used was an experimental teleportation system which had not been thoroughly tested. During the process he sustained multiple injuries to his physical body. The race of beings that had done this had not envisaged this happening.

As soon as he materialised in their world they were horrified to discover that they had almost completely shattered his physical frame. Fortunately, his brain function was still intact. He was immediately placed into a resuscitation unit where he was assessed for a complete bionic alignment. This would enable him to survive in their environment, although it was unlikely that he would ever be able to return to his own world.

As he regained consciousness he sensed he was in the presence of something alien and extraordinary. There was also a feeling of familiarity, that something in this was akin to the visions and dreams that had recently been disturbing him. Even considering how advanced their medical knowledge was, it was a miracle that the creatures were able to stabilise him considering how severely the transportation had injured his body.

It had not been the intention of these creatures to risk harming him and they were horrified to discover how much trauma he had suffered. They immediately summoned their best physicians to attend to him.

To ensure his well being, an Overseer was appointed, and was given the responsibility of introducing him to this new world. It would be an enormous and unprecedented challenge, but they felt that they owed him the best that could be done. Yan was unaware of this and, at present, nothing made sense. As he lay motionless all he could see was a strange bluish light. He was confused and could only make out some of the words that they were saying.

'The alignment was unfortunate.'

'It was unfortunate, but we can still retrieve the data from its cortex if we keep it alive.'

'A suitable biomass will be replicated to replace the damaged organs.'

'All is in hand, but the subject must remain in a conscious state.'

Yan's predicament was causing enormous controversy. This was a serious moral dilemma for his captors. They managed to attend to the physical damage of his traumatised body, but became aware that the healing process would take a long time. Having such a special specimen was very important to them and they felt they were obligated to explain why they had abducted him, although in many ways this had been to them an inexcusable travesty.

He heard a voice say, 'You will exist in a temporal state until we can align and replicate a suitable biomass, this will take time.'

Yan found it impossible to comprehend what was happening. While they explored ways to maintain his physical survival, they had to keep him in an animated state, which meant that he was awake and aware of every moment.

The remit of the Overseer, who was instructed to attend to his psychological needs, was to make him as comfortable as possible. They had to ensure that there would not be any further deterioration of his synapses.

Yan was only aware of the fact that he was in some kind of highly advanced laboratory. This was a specially constructed environment where they could monitor his vital signs and begin the process of realignment.

Their first task was to establish communication. This was enabled via an auditory implant which stimulated his language centre. This would further stimulate his cortex. It was important that he believed he was alive and safe, otherwise his mind would have gone into shock and shut down, rendering it impossible to retrieve the vital information they needed. What was certain was that Yan had to in some way survive. There was much resting on this.

At first Yan's thoughts were random and confused. Everything in his mind seemed jumbled. Then, as time passed, he began to hear a voice that was more directed towards him, and seemed to more closely mimic that of a human. Yan had a mass of questions, but above all he wanted to know where he was and who he was now talking to. The 'voice' introduced itself and a dialogue at last began to take shape. 'My name is Overseer 1. I will be your guide and your friend. Tell me, what is your name?' The voice was distinctly robotic and spoke in a dull monotone. Then it began to adjust its inflection.

Yan found that he could reply and heard himself speak. 'I am Yan, who are you?'

'I am Overseer 1.' Again this seemed a little robotic.

'Where am I?'

'You are in Seronia on the planet Neon, the voice began to synchronise with Yan. This made him feel less panicked but he was utterly overawed.

'Why did you bring me to this place?'

The Overseer had been instructed to not divulge too much at this stage.

'We rescued you from the aqua, you most certainly would have not survived that environment.' This was not quite true, but they felt this might help him comprehend that they meant no harm.

Yan still had no real understanding of what had occurred, but tried to look to his future. 'What will happen to me now?'

'Do not be alarmed, no harm will come to you.'

There was a long pause while certain complex instruments were arranged around him.

'Is there anything that you wish to know?'

'I want to know everything!' There were so many questions in Yan's mind.

The Overseer paused for a moment. Yan became aware of a pulsating light in front of him which began to transmit strange images. He heard thousands of voices all speaking at once.

'Stop!' he screamed in fear.

Almost immediately everything went blank.

'Do not be alarmed. We are trying to give you answers to your questions.'

As Yan had asked to know everything they felt they had to in some way comply. Yan's mind was immediately bombarded with far more information than he could process and he was completely overwhelmed. Some time after the image bombardment had stopped he shouted out again.

'What are you doing to me?'

The Overseer, frustrated with the slow progress of his charge curtly replied, 'You asked to know everything.'

'Yes, but can we take this a little slower!'

Immediately the Overseer then realised his error and frantically readjusted the data portals. He apologised profusely,

'Forgive me I will slow the process so that your inferior brain can accept the information. Where would you like to start?'

'Perhaps the beginning!' Little did Yan know that this was going to take some time. He was not able to absorb the information very well. The Overseer felt agitated, things were not progressing well due to the limited intelligence of this species.

'Where am I?' Yan asked again

Instantly an image was relayed to him in what seemed to be incredibly detailed technicolour. Yan was transfixed.

He saw a beautiful planet bathed in a glowing scarlet hue, orbited by two iridescent moons. Yan was again aware of a sense of familiarity.

'I think I have had dreams about this place, why am I here?'

'We have brought you here to help us in the darkest moment of our history,' it said in a solemn voice.

'I don't understand. Why me?'

'We have been studying your kind for some time now.'

'Oh, you mean you have been studying me?' he snapped, feeling somehow violated.

'You must understand, there is much that we need to explain, about our world, our lives and our planet,' the voice continued.

'Our planet ...' there was a pause as the Overseer seemed to be carefully considering what it would say next, 'evolved in much the same way as yours.'

'I am struggling to comprehend this,' Yan interrupted in

confusion. There was another pause.

The Overseer realised he would need to simplify his explanations and requested the use of a VR. The voice continued its narration. 'This is our planet.' Yan felt himself immediately transported into a virtual landscape of incredible detail.

'In the beginning great rivers scoured the surface, leaving a high plateau which you can see extends for several thousand miles across the surface.'

'It looks immense, but what lies on either side of it?'

The imaging zoomed in on the edges of the plateau.

'Can you see the steep cliffs which drop vertically into the ocean?'

'Yes' replied Yan.

'You will also see that on the landward side again there are great cliffs dropping down to a vast plain.'

Yan was spellbound by the scale of the landscape. It seemed that the cliffs descended for mile after mile.

'How do you get to the bottom?' he was puzzled.

'With great difficulty. It would be an extremely hazardous endeavour to descend below.'

Yan then asked a more perplexing question, 'How is it that you are here?'

The Overseer seemed to sigh. 'As the great waters withdrew, there was an explosion of life. Many different elements combined causing millions of creatures great and small to come into existence. These creatures became adept at adapting to the extremes of the varying habitats.' It then stopped, considering carefully what to say next.

Yan interrupted, 'Yes I understand that, but how?'

The Overseer continued. 'In due course there was

an ascendance of extraordinary intelligent beings who inhabited three distinct domains. They evolved in isolation from one another and fathered three diverse civilisations.'

'You mean three distinct civilisations?' Yan's curiosity was aroused.

The Overseer hesitated for a moment.

'Their evolution was dictated by their unique environments.'

'I don't follow,' said Yan. 'What environments are you talking about?'

The Overseer asked him to look towards the far side of the plateau and said, 'Can you see how our lands are bounded at their furthest points?'

'Ah, that looks very strange!' said Yan. ' It doesn't resemble anything I know.'

The environments were unlike anything on Earth. They were both distinctive and alien, sculpted by powerful and unforgiving forces.

'What do you mean when you say they evolved in isolation from each other?' Yan interrupted again.

The Overseer was at pains to try to make him understand and continued. 'You must appreciate that they were separated by vast and insurmountable physical barriers.'

'Yes, I understand, but when did you finally become aware of each other's existence?'

'It took many thousands of years.'

Yan interrupted, 'I don't understand. How could that happen? Who were these people and how did they live?'

The Overseer paused while he employed a drone to fix Yan's attention on a great mountain range.

'These are the Great Ariane Mountains. They lie at

the furthest reaches of the great plains which spread for thousands of miles before they reach the escarpment – the Seronia Plateau.' He paused again, as if to emphasise the importance of his next statement.

'This great escarpment is the crowning glory of the planet.'

Yan could see that it towered above the plains.

'In what way do you mean this?' he asked.

The Overseer tried to explain. 'We are the Seronians.' Then he paused again. He wasn't sure how much more he should divulge, but Yan insisted on knowing about the other inhabitants.

As the Overseer attempted to relate these facts, he was mindful of Yan's fragile condition. However, as Yan insisted on learning more it was decided that the dialogue should continue. The instruments gathered around him showed that Yan was responding well to the interaction. This was essential if they were to stabilise his vital functions. The Overseer, however, was instructed to simplify the discourse even further in order to accommodate his limited understanding.

'You can see that the cliffs drop into a great ocean. This ocean supports a watery domain which is called Calfaria, and extends from the shores into the depths of the ocean itself.'

'Who lives there?' Yan asked.

'They are an inferior species. You must understand the Domains are unique unto themselves.' The Overseer merely hinted at this insularity. He didn't want to disclose too much yet.

'Interaction and communication between the Domains is not possible.' He then changed the subject and focussed on the topography of Seronia.

'You can see that Seronia and its vast urban areas extend for miles across the flat terrain of the plateau. Our city is an exceptional testament to our engineering and architectural prowess. From ancient times our civilisation and culture has grown at an exponential rate. We are a highly sophisticated and technologically advanced society.'

The vast city of Seronia had a skyline of futuristic high reaching buildings. This metropolis was a testament to their scientific knowhow and their sophisticated technologies. The great city seemed to be constantly buzzing with energy as a network of super highways transported its citizens to and from its central hub.

Yan asked if they ever travelled beyond their city. The answer was a curt 'no'. The Overseer explained that it was rare for a Seronian to venture beyond the city limits because they were used to the artificial environments there which protected them from the harsh external elements.

Yan noticed that the Seronians were physically tall, lean beings with characteristically pale skin. This made them look serene and ethereal, although this was their vulnerability. They would have been unable to withstand the effects of the powerful Neonian sun or survive the extreme temperatures outside.

The skyline of Seronia was dominated by three great 'Orbs'. Yan was fascinated by them. He felt he had seen them before in one of his strange dreams. They had glowing silvery surfaces which shone like metallic beacons. He asked the Overseer to explain what they were.

'These are the domiciles of our esteemed "Directive".'

'What is the Directive?'

The Overseer paused for a while and then said, 'It is an enabling, assistive artificial intelligence.'

'Who controls it?' again the Overseer paused

'The Directive is the servant of the Supreme Council. They are representatives from the highest echelons of our society and are ruled by our "Supreme", known as the "Mahon".'

Every aspect of existence in Seronia was facilitated by the Directive. It was highly efficient and enhanced their daily lives in many ways. It was able to fulfil all the more mundane tasks using its many automatons and it assisted the people in their pursuit of the more refined and aesthetic values such as art, beauty and culture. It could be said that this privileged race had become quite arrogant, tending to display a kind of haughtiness which made them seem cold and aloof.

One particular manifestation of the Directive was a virtual personal assistant for everyone called Cora. It was networked everywhere, from the central facilities to the furthest suburban dwellings. It controlled all aspects of both the recreational facilities and the transport system. 'Cora' could be accessed at any time as it was omnipresent. The Seronians seemed to happily embrace the intrusion, their lives being constantly directed and informed by it.

The Overseer noticed that Yan's vital signs indicated that he was moving dangerously into overload. He felt that for the moment this was as much as Yan could absorb. It was decided that he should now be sedated and carefully monitored. Having got so far they couldn't risk further deterioration of his faculties. They would then re-evaluate him when they were satisfied he was able to continue.

# THE DOMAINS

It would take a long time to explain to Yan the complicated history of the unique civilisations that occupied the great Domains. For generations they had lived in almost complete isolation from one another due to the vast distances and physical barriers between them. The Overseer was instructed not to give away too much information. There were unresolved disputes concerning their territorial boundaries.

The Seronians first discovered the Calfarians quite accidentally. A ferocious earthquake of unprecedented magnitude occurred and exposed a vast chasm on the eastern side of the plateau. Further explorations revealed long winding tunnels which led to huge caves opening onto a rocky beach. A group of shore - dwelling Calfarian farmers had made a temporary camp in the caves. They were discovered by a team of Seronians who were assessing the stability of the area. They greeted the Seronians with friendliness and curiosity. They were not too dissimilar in appearance to themselves, apart from a couple of crucial adaptations which enabled them to breathe underwater and to tolerate a greater degree of pressure.

Calfaria was a region that occupied a huge area of the great ocean that covered at least a third of the planet. This was divided into four great sectors. These were referred to as the Great Depths, the Channels, the Levels, and the Shallows.

In the Great Depths there was an ancient underwater city. It rose from the sea bed like a sculptured coral reef. The buildings were carved from a calciferous material which possessed some remarkable qualities. During the daytime, rays of the Neonian sun penetrated the depths and cast diffuse rainbows of light all around them. At night the illumination from the two moons stimulated the reflective calcites of the buildings, causing them to emit a soft warm fluorescent glow. This was a place of unparalleled beauty and the home of a great underwater nation.

The reason the Seronians had little or no knowledge of the existence of Calfaria was because it was hidden behind a great wall of solid water that could not be penetrated. The Calfarians had discovered how to manipulate the properties of water, enabling them to protect and hide their cities from unwelcome visitors. This invisible barrier could not be punctured or pierced. The only way through was via the aqua tunnels which could only be opened by the Guardians.

If the Seronians had understood the true nature of the Calfarian shore people and their special abilities, they might have refrained from the course of action that they eventually pursued. What they did glean was that these people were farming offshore, under the water. In fact, they only ventured onto the shoreline itself during the 'harvest', which occurred every four years.

They farmed a kelp that grew in the Shallows, which was a very important crop. It was very versatile and was an important food which had sustained them for centuries.

The stringy filaments of the stems had properties which made them very useful as they were both pliable and extremely strong.

The crop was farmed using traditional methods which had not changed for centuries. They adhered strictly to a rotational cycle of growth. It could only be harvested at the moment of the rising moon. As the silvery rays dissipated into the aqua the crop would suddenly blossom, at which point they would swiftly gather it and stack it to dry it on the rocks. Later they would store it in the caves ready for transport back to the great city.

The Seronians grew curious about the kelp. They wanted to know why the farmers worked so hard to gather it. They managed to secure some samples of it and took it back to Seronia for analysis. To their astonishment they found it to be highly nutritious. They were then directed to form some kind of trade relationship with the Calfarians in order to secure supplies.

At first the relationship was amicable. Trade deals were established for small amounts. However, the Seronians began to demand more and more. It seemed they developed an insatiable appetite for it. Unfortunately, the farmers did not have the means to meet their demands.

The Seronians tried hard to capitalise on the opportunity to acquire this highly nutritious and popular product. They used their powers of persuasion to manipulate the Calfarians into supplying greater amounts by offering them irresistible incentives.

The kelp was exchanged for access to the outer reaches of Seronia. The sophisticated leisure and recreational facilities which they were given access to in these areas were so compelling that the 'Shore' people became completely enamoured. The consequence was that they wanted to remain longer and longer in these distractions. Consequently they were less willing to return to Calfaria. This allowed the Seronians to pursue this new product with a vengeance. They began to mechanise the harvest and extensively farm it. They continued to manipulate the farmers by offering them permanent residences along the shore line. With the farmers staying for much longer periods in the fields, the Seronian were able to increase the yields from the farms. It became a vicious circle of tempting inducements.

The Seronians, in their eagerness to manipulate the Calfarians into supplying more and more kelp, had severely misjudged their true nature. By remaining for longer periods away from their homelands they began to lose touch with their own people and culture. As their farms began to expand from the Shallows into the Levels, they intruded into previously forbidden territory, and disturbed the delicate harmony of this environment. The changes that were being made were far too radical. The expansion of kelp farming resulted in the decimation of many other species. This then caused dismay and anger in Calfaria.

There were other issues too. The caves were connected to Seronia via a myriad of tunnels, which the Calfarians would on occasion use in order to venture into zones of the city that were forbidden to them. The attempts of the Seronians to confine and restrict these incursions caused great discontent, and no compromise could be found.

The other great Domain was located to the far west of Seronia, and was known as Tharmenia. To reach it from

Seronia was an epic journey. The descent from the plateau itself was treacherous and the vast plain that led to the outskirts was inhospitable and dangerous. It occupied one of the most remote regions of the planet. The Tharmenians were adapted to a harsher, more physically demanding life in the high snow-capped mountains and valleys. Despite this, they were a prodigious, remarkable race of people.

Physically they were small in stature, strong and incredibly agile. Their skin was a dark violet colour, which gave them protection from the harsh rays of the Neonian sun. Being nimble and light on their feet enabled them to easily negotiate the mountainous terrain, and they could scale the steepest crags with incredible speed.

For thousands of years they had carved out an existence which was more or less nomadic. During the long hot summer season they wandered the plains. The winters though were extremely cold and harsh, so during this season they took shelter inside the caves of the mountains.

These were people who totally lived by their faith. They experienced a conscious knowledge of a divinity which they termed the 'Terra'. They worshipped this with unparalleled devotion and drew their inspiration from the words of their ancestors. They were essentially metaphysical, so much so that divinity was attributed to certain advanced individuals who manifested a distinctively coloured emanation. Those who had 'ascended' were imbued with a shining golden aura.

The holy lands of the Tharmenians were located in the Ariane Mountains which rose steeply towering above the plains. Their peaks rose high into the sky and wisps of clouds snaked around their craggy ridges. One mountain seemed to reach higher than the rest. Its peak dominated the skyline. This was the holy mountain of 'Araby'. This mountain held a great secret. It was there that the fabled 'Labyrinth' could be found.

# THE GREAT CHANGE

It was the Great 'C' that had threatened Seronia in the past. This was the most catastrophic event that the planet had ever experienced. The 'Great Catastrophe', or 'Great C' as it came to be known, originated in the darkest recesses of space. It was caused by a cosmic tsunami emanating from the collision of two neutron stars. Neon, being the ninth most distant planet in the Triangulum System, was to bear the brunt of its destructive power.

It began to suffer calamitous changes. The trizone layer was heavily eroded, causing the Neonian sun to penetrate the atmosphere with greater ferocity.

Seronia became highly vulnerable to solar radiation. Their high position on the plateau exposed them constantly to the sun's bombardment.

The city suffered also from severe solar contamination, which decomposed the fabric of buildings and thinned the atmosphere at an alarming rate, threatening their very existence. Drastic action was needed, and their greatest engineers and scientists were called upon to find a way to protect them.

An innovator of exceptional talent called Tostare was selected to head the project. He proposed an extraordinary engineering concept. He had gained considerable success with a material which incorporated the living filaments of the Calfarian kelp. Dwellings along the shore were built with it and housed the Calfarian farmers. The structures were so strong that they were even able to withstand the ravages of pounding waves and ferocious storms. They were basically 'living houses' which were supported by structures that were also living.

His proposal was to construct a great dome over the entire city, supported on plinths constructed from this organic material. The problem that still remained was that a compound suitable for the dome itself had not yet been synthesised. The kelp filaments were ideal for the plinths, but a material which was both light and transparent and yet strong enough to withstand the solar corrosion of the scorching sun had still to be found.

Thousands of scientists scoured data banks and experimented with multitudes of different materials to no avail. The Directive extended its search beyond the city itself in the hope of locating exotic materials which their science had not yet discovered. During this process many outreach institutions on the very edge of Tharmenia were contacted. Some of these institutions functioned, among other things, as bio-realignment foundations. It was here, well away from civilised society, that certain 'unfortunate' offspring were sent from the procreation units of Seronia.

Procreation in Seronia had long been a sanitised procedure. They did not leave anything to chance, ensuring that the product of their reproductive processes were of the highest 'quality'. 'Foetuses' were nurtured in specially adapted environments and were born in artificial birthing stations. They were only assigned to parents after many checks had ensured they were perfect. On rare occasions, problems did occur. If babies displayed any developmental issues they would usually be realigned. Ninety-nine per cent of the time this was successful, but sometimes the realignment failed. When this occurred, it was necessary to find a suitable home for the 'unfortunate'. They were placed in outreach establishments, known as BRF domiciles. They were often located on the very edge of the city and sometimes beyond. One such was located close to the boundary of Tharmenia

Here a handful of them resided. They were all known as G specimens, denoting the year of their birth. This letter was followed by an individual code which designated their particular irregularities on a numerical scale. The higher the number the more serious the problem. G190 seemed to have inherited a rare xz gene. He was hypersensitive in many respects, with extraordinary hearing and eyesight. Although he was very different in appearance from Seronian norms, he was well built, but quite small and angular in stature. He had piercing eyes and a distinct jaw. With such attributes, it had been difficult to decide what tasks to assign him to.

Despite the oddities of his appearance, it was recognised that certain aspects of his intelligence bordered on genius. After much deliberation about his future it was felt that he should remain at the BRF permanently as a very useful asset.

The BRF's primary function was that of an important 'seed depositary', for a range of biodiverse specimens. It was there that G190 was given a position as a researcher. Here he worked on the identification of local plant species and gained much credit for his meticulous observations.

It was when he began to extend his research into the uncharted areas encroaching the Tharmenian border that his findings revealed more than he expected. In the process he also encountered the Tharmenians themselves. To his surprise they were very friendly and accepting of him. His appearance was of no consequence to them, in fact, they applauded his physical strength and agility. As he became more familiar he became fascinated by them. They came to trust him and allowed him to freely mingle with them.

One particularly cold morning G190 ventured further than usual and found himself in a valley surrounded by high-peaked jagged mountains. He found himself following a path which seemed to end at a craggy cliff. He kept going because wanted to see if he could find a 'blue sapphire'. He had seen a picture of a specimen in the seed registry, and had been enamoured with it. It was a unique and rare flower, similar to a daisy but with iridescent blue petals of transcendent beauty.

As he made his way along the perilous slippery path, to his amazement he spotted one. As he was about to reach down and pluck it from its stem, a hand slapped him on the wrist from behind, and he heard a voice cry, 'Bah, don't touch the shining one, she will lose her lustre!'

He was so taken aback he nearly fell off the ledge. In an instant someone grabbed him and pulled him to safety.

'You be who?' the being asked.

'I'm G190,' he replied.

'I've never met a G190!' he laughed gently.

'Come, come here, sit with me and tell me all about yourself.'

He beckoned him to come forward. G 190 was quite shy and reserved, having had little experience of conversation with strangers. He stood awkwardly, unsure of how to proceed. 'Well let me introduce myself, I am Baliya.'

Baliya did not understand the G190 delineation and scratched his head in puzzlement.

'Why are you called G190?'

'Well, I'm genetically, well they tell me I'm a misfit, a mismatch or something.' He hung his head down in shame and embarrassment.

Baliya was taken aback, 'Come, come look at me, what am I?'

He jumped up and down patting his wobbly belly and laughing. He was a little rotund creature, with long grey hair, grey beard and deep soulful eyes.

'I'm not sure. Who and what are you?'

He felt he sounded a little rude but then began to feel slightly in awe of the strange little creature which was staring at him. He noticed that there was something of an aura, a brightness around him. The creature rocked from side to side.

'I am Baliya!' he began to laugh loudly again.

He instantly liked him and felt comfortable. Little did he know he was in the presence of the supreme spiritual leader of Tharmenia. He was somewhat overwhelmed and felt a sense of belonging that was new to him.

'I am grateful for your acceptance,' he said modestly.

'You should not need acceptance, surely we are now friends.'

He became anxious, but quickly Baliya lifted his spirits.

'Well, my friends have names and so shall you, hmm ...

I think I will name you G, G for Gathine, and from now on everyone should call you by your name, yes?'

'Really? Yes, why not? Yes my name could be Gathine.' He suddenly smiled and seemed to feel taller.

'How can I make others say my name?' he suddenly looked sad again.

'Well, perhaps the future will change everything, your name will be known by many!' Baliya reassured him. He possessed the gift of prophecy.

It had not occurred to Gathine that anything could ever change in his life. The foundation was all he had known and he had learned to accept his role there. However, as the weeks went by, he ventured further and further into Tharmenia. He began to identify more closely with them and their way of life. His work had given him the opportunity to spend time in their environment and this was where he now found contentment. Gathine and Baliya's relationship blossomed too. Baliya had a profound liking for him as well as a sadness for his predicament. Baliya was curious about his work.

'What do you do at this foundation?' he asked one day as they were sitting in a small dell.

'I collect biomaterials and seeds. I'm working on these samples.' Gathine opened his bag full of seeds and plants.

'Yes, I can see that you are a seed collector, that's how our ancestors survived.'

'Ancestors, that's very interesting, what did they collect?'

Instead of replying, Baliya beckoned Gathine to follow him along a path which led to the opening of a cave halfway up the mountain. The outside of the cave was festooned with all kinds of adornments. It was obvious this was a special place.

'Here we are, this is the holy cave of the ancients.'

Baliya made a few symbolic gestures to an image that was painted on the wall of the cave.

'This is where our people brought their families, in ancient times. Be careful where you tread.'

Baliya seemed to skip along a precarious path leading deeper into the cave. There were tunnels going off in various directions. It was the labyrinth.

Baliya led him up some steps that had been hewn from the rocks to an opening in the cave wall. Through it he could see a magnificent view below.

'This is the promised land, our land, your land.' They sat for quite some time contemplating the landscape.

Gathine realised he could learn much from Baliya. He knew instinctively that there was something special about him. He discovered that he was very old, at least two hundred years, and yet was still full of irrepressible energy. He spent many hours discussing the esoteric aspects of life with him. He learned that the Tharmenians had various 'deities', but their real nature eluded him.

On one particular grey damp morning, he was wandering along the valley gathering grass seeds when he became mesmerised by a strange and pungent odour which seemed to overwhelm him. Following its trail, he entered a dark little dell. In the midst of it he came upon a pond surrounded by a thick reed bed. There seemed to be some kind of activity apparent around the edges. He pushed his way through the reeds and edged closer and closer. He saw what seemed to be concentric circles emanating across the pond, indicating some kind of vibration, and the air was filled with a high-pitched humming sound. The circles started to resonate in sequence with the humming, which gradually increased in volume.

At that point he was amazed to see the water begin to glow. A strange mist appeared and hung heavily just above the surface. He learned afterwards that he had witnessed the spawning of a 'Rosanthrocae' plant, which only occurred once every four years. At the height of this activity the lake was completely covered by a glowing luminescent film. Gathine was transfixed, but had the presence of mind to reach into the pool and take a sample.

On his return to the BRF he made an analysis of it, submitting his findings to the Institute. He was completely unaware of the fact that he just encountered the most holy deity of the Tharmenian people.

He kept the sample in a secure container in his laboratory. It fascinated him and he would spend hours staring at it, transfixed by its rippling glow. In the eyes of the Tharmenians, however, he had made a terrible transgression. Rosanthrocae was a sacred organism with certain extraordinary properties. Its existence had been kept secret for thousands of years because in the wrong hands its properties could be dangerous. It had a power far beyond his scientific understanding. By taking a sample of it, he had violated and disrespected the Tharmenian 'Ancestors'.

Baliya was saddened by this violation and refused to grant him any further audiences. Unfortunately for Gathine, he did not understand the nature of his misdemeanour. He gradually retreated back into himself and rarely left the foundation, uneasily burying himself in his work in order to forget the happiness he had lost.

# THE IMPOSITION

Some years later Gathine was busy cataloguing a specimen called 'sylvaticum maxim' when he heard a strange whirring noise. He went to the window and looked outside. In the quad bay a shuttle transport vehicle from Seronia had arrived. This was highly unusual as they rarely saw visitors from Seronia, just the usual supply shuttles. As the doors slid open, two enforcement trooper androids from Seronia appeared. They were met by the overseer of the foundation.

'This is not the supply shuttle, what is your business here?

'We have a subpoena for G190,' was the reply.

'Surely not, this must be a mistake.'

The overseer was taken aback, as nothing like this had ever happened before. The androids looked quite menacing and were not prepared to discuss the matter.

'No mistake, we require access to the bio depositary,' was their curt reply.

The overseer tried in vain to redirect them

'This is all very irregular!'

He was disturbed by their harshness as they pushed him out of the way and headed for the bio dorm where Gathine was working. Without preamble, he was ordered to attend the Supreme Council immediately. They also confiscated his Rosanthrocae sample.

Gathine was manhandled into the back of the transporter and the journey began.

The transit across the long plains was long and uncomfortable. He pressed his face against the window of the transporter, looking back towards the only life he had ever known. In the distance he could see the towering peaks of the mountains. He was sad to leave the foundation and felt a premonition that he would never return to the Tharmenia he had grown to love.

Gradually, the transporter climbed the edges of the great plateau, heading ever upwards towards the lights of the great city. It was eventually guided onto the landing area of the Great Orb. He was then led from the transporter along echoing corridors into a holding area. This was a highly disturbing experience for Gathine. He was met by a 'guide' android who escorted him to another room where he sat nervously on the edge of his seat, his heart pounding. Another individual entered. Tostare sat down wordlessly opposite Gathine. In the silence they studied each other.

Tostare was dressed in formal attire. He looked disconcerted by this strange little individual, perched on the edge of his seat looking down at the floor. He spoke first.

'I'm not familiar with your kind, where are you from?'

Gathine looked around and felt anxious. He gathered up his cloak and tried to stand tall. Then a feeling of desperation seemed to overcome him.

'Can't talk, need ... got ... to go!'

Tostare began to realise how disruptive this whole experience must have been.

Tostare was a kind and thoughtful being, and he tried to put Gathine at ease.

'My name is Tostare, what's yours?'

Gathine was proud to reveal his name and stood proudly saying, 'I'm Gathine, G A T H I N E.'

He shouted it as loud as he could. Then he felt afraid. 'I don't like this place, I want to go now.'

With that he gave out a loud and terrified howl and began to run around the room seeking an exit. Tostare was shaken. He had never seen anyone remotely like this before. 'Come, come, it's alright, sit here next to me.' He spoke kindly.

Gathine began to calm down a little.

'There, there, that wasn't so difficult was it?' Gathine sensed that Tostare was not hostile and recovered himself. 'Sorry, but this is very difficult for me.'

'And me,' Tostare smiled at him.

'What do they want?'

'I presume it's got something with my design for the city.'

'But they have taken my treasure, what do they want with it?'

Tostare again tried to placate him. 'Well, it's not everyone that gets called to the Chamber, it's a great honour!'

'I wasn't called, I was dragged here by them.' He pointed towards two troopers who were standing in the alcove.

'Hmm, that doesn't sound right.'

Gathine was gripped with a wave of panic and held onto Tostare's arm. Owing to his strength the grip was very uncomfortable. He was getting more and more distressed and shouted, 'Why am I here? Why do you presume I care about your city? You have brought me here against my will. Return me immediately!'

At that moment a screen began to illuminate around them and a voice addressed them both.

'Welcome, Tostare and G190,'

There was a pause. Gathine raised his fist and shouted again at the screen

'I have a name, do you hear me? A NAME, and that is GATHINE.'

He began to run around the room shouting his name over and over again. The voice attempted a more reasonable tone in order to calm him.

'Apologies, welcome Gathine.' Gathine stood still and stared at the screen. 'You have been summoned here for reasons which are of the utmost importance. We are facing an unprecedented crisis.'

Gathine was looking extremely agitated.

The communication continued. 'Our city and our civilisation are our only destiny. We must protect them at all costs.'

Tostare felt apprehensive. He glanced towards the entrance and saw that it was guarded by a trooper droid. This was not what he was expecting. He felt something was wrong.

There was silence. Tostare felt both perplexed and worried as he detected an air of menace in the voice.

# THE EXPERIMENT

The AI Directive that oversaw the Supreme Council had issued Protocol 1. This meant that the situation had moved in classification from a severe to an immediate threat. The emergency services were now activated. An evacuation of the city began. The people were being bunkered into survival chambers below the city. They would have to remain there for the foreseeable future unless something could save the city from further disintegration. It was a frightening and difficult time as nobody had no idea what the future would hold.

The Directive had instigated supra mode, shutting down anything that was unnecessary and directing all the surplus energy into its systems. In the main chamber the Supreme Council was waiting anxiously for the Mahon.

The Directive's search had been its most extensive to date. The system itself was in extreme overload. Data from every access point had been analysed, even those in the outreach systems. This was a last attempt to source a suitable compound for Tostare's proposed dome structure. It cross matched thousands of specimens.

At this point it had made a bizarre discovery. A unique amoebic eukaryotic organism had recently been added to the bio directory. It turned out to be a compound found in the Rosanthrocae plant that Gathine had been studying. Under normal circumstances, many tests would have taken place to ensure its suitability for the task, but the initial indications were that it would satisfy all the criteria. In normal circumstances it would take years to conduct all the necessary calculations and research in order to perfect the dome material, but no more time was available. A radical new proposal was suggested, whereby the intellects of both Tostare and Gathine were combined in an interface that would utilise the AI capabilities of the Directive. The technology that would enable this had never been tried before and was considered to be highly risky.

The Mahon was charged with presenting this plan to the Supreme Council.

'This process is highly dangerous! Can the joining of the neural synapses of two separate beings ever be justified?' argued one of the councillors.

'There is no other course of action as there is no time left.'

The Mahon was silent for a few minutes, then raised his head and addressed the assembly.

'The end justifies the means!'

There was a silence as each member of the council cast a vote to decide the fate of Gathine and Tostare.

They had concluded that this was the correct path to take.

Meanwhile, Gathine and Tostare were detained in the chamber.

'What's going on, why are we here?' Gathine grabbed Tostare.

Tostare looked around the room. All exits were now

guarded. As he approached them, a trooper stood firmly in front of him, barring the way.

'Something feels wrong.' Tostare's voice quivered. 'I demand an explanation, why I have been brought to the Chamber!'

A voice echoed, 'You are here to serve!'

The next thing that they knew was that they were being escorted to a side chamber. The doors were sealed behind them.

They were encircled by androids and placed on adjacent platforms. They were held face down, and their heads immobilised with clamps. A multitude of sensors were fixed permanently to their skulls, utilising a complex nest of wires to connect to huge banks of machinery lining the walls of the chamber. Their arms and legs were also secured. As fluid was intravenously pumped into their bodies they drifted into a semiconscious state, lying motionless, unable to speak.

At this point they became aware of each other's thoughts. It was apparent that their individual consciousness was being merged. At this point, the interface with the AI Directive was activated.

Within nanoseconds, their individual intellects were absorbed, and a super intelligence began to evolve within the machinery of the Directive. The absorption of Tostare and Gathine's knowledge and combined consciousness improved its capabilities to a staggering degree. Within hours it had finalised Tostare's plans for a protective dome to encapsulate the city. Within days it had successfully modified the compound that had been selected as the building material.

What it conceived was audacious. The Rosanthrocae compound was further enhanced in order to accelerate the speed at which it could be grown. This newly modified material was now produced in enormous quantities. It was then dispersed into the air above the city where it expanded like a huge balloon, enclosing the space below. As it descended it adhered perfectly to the great plinths. The dome turned out to be completely impenetrable to the deadly rays of the Neonian sun. The Seronians were now able to return to their city under its extraordinary canopy knowing that they were safe again.

Life returned to normal, but not for Gathine and Tostare. It was impossible to detach them from the interface, and so there they remained, suspended in deep animation, their synapses connected forever to the matrix of the Directive. The Mahon and senior members of the Council decided to quietly immortalise them, keeping them as they were, entombed in a secret chamber like latter-day pharaohs. Responsibility for their care through the centuries was handed to a small sect known as the Sentinels. And so, Seronia averted the Catastrophe.

The Seronians were, however, unaware of the fact that the Directive continued to evolve, its vastly enhanced functionality allowing it to progress far beyond its previous limits.

# THE IRREGULARITY

For the time being, disaster had been averted. The 'dome' that now enveloped their beautiful city seemed to emanate a lustrous and radiant glow.

Many years passed, new generations lived beneath the dome. Nobody ever ventured beyond it.

The Directive became a different entity altogether. On the one hand, it continued to serve them, but now it had a counter objective. It was not a soulless machine now, it had evolved. It also began to experience a dilemma concerning its own identity. To this end it began to construct a separate world, which it named Etherea. It was a construct within the network that allowed it to interface with a myriad of virtual identities and locations. As time passed it became so immersed in its own creations that it became distracted and in the process began to neglect its primary functions, the most important of which was the constant monitoring of the dome's condition. Almost by chance a procedure initiated by a building droid brought to the attention of the presiding Mahon that there was something unusual occurring in the fifth quadrant of the dome. Immediately, an investigation was launched to find out what the source of the problem was. The results caused extreme concern.

There seemed to be various fissures in the dome. It

looked as though they were radiating from the plinths, and unchecked they would compromise the structure itself.

The Mahon called the Supreme Council to an emergency meeting. There would be several representatives from the science and engineering faculty who would be giving their appraisal of the situation.

The Mahon began the proceedings. It was all very covert. They did not want to raise the alarm for fear of panicking the people.

'We must present our findings to the Directive. Please enter your data into the portals.'

He stood in the centre of the main chamber. On his signal a series of screens illuminated. The information was transmitted and immediately analysed. There was a sudden silence ...

The Mahon was then called into the inner chamber. He beckoned the assembled group to stand down from the portals and await further instructions.

The Mahon stood motionless as a beam of light seemed to engulf him. He remained there for some time. When he emerged his face looked ashen. He summoned the Council to the main podium.

'We stand on the threshold of the ultimate challenge. We must engage our technologies to enable further exploration into the unknown. The molecular structure of the dome is weakening!'

He was interrupted by a councillor, 'What does this mean?'

'It means that the dome seems to have contracted some kind of virus which is compromising the structure.'

'What does the Directive suggest?'

'The Directive suggests that an antiviral is required.'

'Surely we can synthesise a compound?'

'Unfortunately that would not be possible as the virus seems to have emanated from beyond our planet. We must search for a comparative alien compound.'

'There is no viable life in the immediate planets.'

'We will look further, the quantum ports must be made ready.'

'Are you suggesting that we authorise their use before testing them?'

Another voice spoke out. 'We are still unsure of the alignment of the quantum accelerator.'

But before he could finish the Mahon shot him a stern reply. 'The accelerator will be enhanced and engaged!'

He evaded any other questioning. There would be no further discussion.

The Seronians possessed a thorough knowledge of their immediate solar system, but travel beyond this had so far eluded them. The development of quantum ports seemed to now offer the best hope of further exploration of the universe. The ability to tunnel underneath conventional space at quantum level seemed almost within reach. A working prototype had been developed that seemed to vastly progress this technology. There was little doubt that exploration into distant galaxies would at last be possible. The Directive was at the heart of all the developments. As it continued to evolve, its insatiable curiosity on the question of what lies beyond began to preoccupy it more and more. It had become bored, and now had an appetite for adventure. Exploring the universe would allow it to expand its knowledge and seek out new domains.

The quantum 'V', as it was known, was a new technology. The preliminary investigations utilised probes which had the ability to instantaneously teleport both living creatures and inanimate material. Initially, however, they used the beam as a probe which enabled an observer to study remotely. This they transmitted to various test sites. It was a chance encounter that they discovered Earth. If the trajectory path had deviated by even just one Planck length, they would have missed it. The prototype used during early research directed its beam into the Manes Sea completely by accident. They found that the probe could investigate the sea bed quite easily and relay information accurately back to Seronia.

They discovered that this 'aqua', their term for sea and ocean, had an abundance of living organisms that were comparable with their own planet. Initial surveys of the upper layers of the sea bed had located a subterranean cave system that happened to occur directly beneath the Emerald Rocks. It turned out to have perfect conditions for further quantum exchanges. In time it could serve as a portal between the two planets.

The quantum probe was further enhanced with a supramorphing ability. This enabled the operator to manipulate the molecular structure of the immediate surroundings. They were able to transform and mould nearby material and project their own awareness into it. In this aquatic environment they created watery androids of incredible agility. This enabled them to conduct all manner of research without having to impact on any local species. If they were disturbed or detected at any time they could dissipate and no trace would be visible. They did not want to interact with any other species and cause alarm, although they did not anticipate the insatiable curiosity of human beings. One Swedish research scientist in particular.

The Directive had a vested interest in finding a new world to infiltrate. The fact was that it had become disenchanted with its role as the servant of Neon. It had ambitions of its own.

# AN OUT OF BODY EXPERIENCE

Back on planet Earth, events plodded along uneventfully, particularly in the village of Port Lar. Ben, Yan's son, was growing up just like any other teenager. He was reaching a pivotal moment in his life, his GCSE exams were almost over and he was relieved to get home from school. He threw his school bags into the hall. He wanted to avoid an interrogation by his mother, who was on her way down the stairs. More importantly he just wanted to go out with his mates. There wasn't a lot to do in the village. Most likely they would just hang around riding their bikes and challenge each other to all kinds of dares.

His mother called to him, 'Well, how did it go?'

'Fine, ok, just going out.'

'Ben ... BEN!' But before she could get a reply he had headed for the shed and jumped on his bike. He rode without a care down the hill and into the main road of the village, narrowly missing a white van. The driver leaned out of the window shaking his fist shouting, 'You bloody moron!'

Ben ignored him and continued on his way. He wanted to get to the bus shelter before the other kids returned from school. The bus shelter was where the lads from the village hung out. Ben had spent many a night there. The previous night they had been fooling around as usual, playing pranks on each other. Nothing escaped their attention. From that vantage point they could keep their eyes on the whole village. Gossip was rife. Robbie was Ben's best mate, they felt comfortable in each other's company. Robbie had always looked up to Ben. He always had some story or joke to tell. He was a round-faced kid, red haired with freckles and glasses. He was always cheerful.

'Let's wind up Colin!' said Robbie.

Colin was in charge of the gardens but he took his job far too seriously. He was a strange little man. He always wore a checked shirt, corduroy trousers and a scruffy tank top. He had a somewhat bulbous face with protruding teeth. He would turn a reddish purple when he was angry and would literally spit his venom at the perpetrators. This would often lead to a stand-off between him and the local youths who delighted in teasing him.

'Don't be daft. Colin! No, oh alright, should be a laugh!'

They grinned mischievously and raced through the flower beds of the gardens. Colin had spied on them and began his well-practised lambast.

'I'm gonna report you! Got your names!, you're in for it this time you little hooligans!'

He began to run after them waving his spade. It was futile, they criss-crossed the path and fled. The exertion was too much for Colin. He coughed and sputtered and made his way back to the flower bed where he had been laying an immaculate row of marigolds.

Ben and Robbie's usual topics for discussion were stories about cars and fishing, interspersed with the odd account of who had the best tactic of approaching Amy.

She was the girl considered to be the 'fittest' in the village. Apart from her obvious qualities, she was adventurous and full of laughter. Ben liked Amy. He was immensely proud of his friendship with her. They had been in the same class at school so he had known her all of his life. Ben was very excited to tell of his latest escapade.

'I went to Amy's yesterday!' Ben was beaming with excitement

'How did you manage that?' enquired Robbie

'And I saw the Audi Quattro!'

Robbie interrupted 'Nah!, you're joking.'

'AND I had a ride in it,' Ben grinned with pride.

'You jammy git, how did you manage that!' Robbie looked peeved.

Amy's dad, Mike, owned the local garage 'Mike's Wheels'. He was a keen rally driver, owning the most wanted vehicle in the village, a souped-up Audi Quattro

To get even a glimpse of it was regarded as an honour.

'I just got talking to her and asked about the car, she told me to go to the garage and she would ask her dad to show me it.'

'I gotta hand it to you, Ben, you got real skill.' He smiled with genuine approval.

Ben continued, 'Aw! You should have seen it, man, it was so cool!'

He continued to describe the car, how the orange and red bodywork was embellished with a gleaming silver spoiler.

Amy had a soft spot for Ben. She had primed her dad that she had invited him because he was keen to see the car. Her dad saw no harm in him either.

When he had arrived at the garage looking so awestruck, Mike couldn't help but say,

'Would you like to sit in the passenger seat, son?'

'That would be really cool!' He could hardly believe his luck.

Mike had climbed into the driver's seat, and Amy got in the back. At that moment there was a roar from the engine. Ben sat back in the passenger seat, listening intently to the unique throbbing roar of the five-cylinder engine. Beaming all the while, Mike had taken them for a quick spin down the lanes and back.

That experience had been a high point of his childhood. He felt honoured that Amy had let him have that opportunity. Although he wasn't confident enough to consider himself to be in the running for her affections, he had wanted to tell Robbie and his friends about his ride. Unfortunately, he became acutely embarrassed when Robbie teased him about it.

'Ben loves Amy, Ben loves Amy.'

'Shut Up Robbie!' He was decidedly irritated by his suggestion.

Their bantering was halted when they saw the menacing shape of Tooley approaching them.

Tooley wasn't really accepted by the group as he was always in some kind of trouble. He sported a Mohican hairstyle which accented his aggressive appearance. He always seemed to have a sly, calculating expression on his face. It was immediately apparent that his intention wasn't good. He always seemed threatening, and this time it looked like he was going to have a face-off with one of them or that he was going to involve them in yet more vandalism. This made everyone nervous. He was the one who had smashed all the windows of the old pottery workshop. He had also set fire to the grassy bank by the beach, although he had never owned up to it.

'Hey lads, look what I've got for youse all' He smirked as he produced a large, scruffily rolled-up cigarette, which he handed to them. He also produced a lighter.

'Right lads, take a toke on that, well if you dare!' He grinned menacingly.

Gingerly, they did as he bade and passed the 'spliff' around, each taking a puff. The more inexperienced smokers began to splutter and cough. Tooley then wandered off, still with that shifty look on his face.

Before the 'spliff' reached Ben, one of them spied the local copper wandering down the road.

'Quick, put it in the wall,' someone shouted. From being like bees that had been around a honey pot they were startled, and now flew off in different directions on their bikes. Their skilful manoeuvres were practised and graceful as they sped off down the narrow winding lanes.

Ben was the only one who hadn't had a turn, and it disturbed him that he had missed out on the experience. He had the distinct feeling that this could affect his cred with the group. He resolved that he would go back the next day and retrieve it.

He rode off down the road back to his house. It looked strange, spookily silhouetted against the sky. It was a large ramshackle sort of place which in its heyday had been quite grandiose. Barging the front door open, he headed for the kitchen, and more particularly the fridge. He pulled open the door roughly and a carton of milk toppled and spilled all over the floor. He grabbed a tea towel, wiped a bit of it up and then drank what was left. He ungraciously stuffed some cheese into his mouth, almost choking while swallowing it. He ran upstairs to his bedroom but tiptoed along the landing past his mother's bedroom. He then saw that the door of his brother's bedroom was open. He peered in and saw a packet of Hobnobs on a pile of old CDs. This was an opportunity not to be missed. He grabbed a handful and retreated to his own room to devour them.

That night as he lay in his bed, his mind was full of anticipation and curiosity. He furtively planned his retrieval of the spliff from the wall. He woke up early and peered through his bedroom curtains, noticing the sun just beginning to rise above the sea on the horizon. Its rays lit up the bay with a luminous orange glow.

He got dressed and grabbed his green khaki jacket. He liked this jacket, bought from the little fishing shop in Port Lar. It had a distinctly pungent odour, probably because he had shoved fish into the deep pockets from time to time. His mum had tried to wash it on various occasions but he had always managed to rescue it from the washing basket, in order to preserve its oily waterproofing. He then slipped quietly down the stairs. He headed for the kitchen and tried to quietly sneak through the back door. Grace, Ben's mother, had been awoken by the sound of the door banging against its frame. Usually it took two shoves and a hitch to get it to close properly. Recent storms played havoc with hinges and she hadn't gotten around to getting it fixed. She called down, 'Ben is that you?'

He called back, 'I'm just going to Robbie's, we're off fishing!'

He knew he needed to get out quickly before he was asked to do something. His mother shouted, 'Ben, I need you to get some milk; there's some change in the dish on the dresser.' Her voice sounded weak and faded.

'Oh shit, shit shit!' Ben muttered in irritation. He rushed back and grabbed the coins, stuffing them into his jacket pocket.

'Ok, see you later, Mum.' He left the house without further interruptions, mounted his bike and headed down the road.

He pedalled furiously as he needed to get to the local shop as quickly as possible. He exchanged a few awkward comments with the shopkeeper, a bearded biker who always wore a 'Black Nazareth' T shirt. He had crooked yellowing teeth and a grizzled face, which had earned him the nickname Pirate J. He was fond of Ben's mother and always tried to endear himself to Ben.

'So how's school, Ben?' This was the last thing he wanted to talk about.

'Have you got a girlfriend yet?' Another annoying question,

'No way!' Ben replied shyly, to which Pirate J just laughed.

He handed Ben the bread and milk and took the grubby coins from his hand. It was plain that Pirate J wasn't yet done with his clumsy efforts to glean information about his mother. 'How's your mum doing? I could drop by if she needs ...'

Before he could finish his sentence Ben was out of the shop. He had other things on his mind. He headed for the bus shelter. Thankfully no one was around. He fumbled around the wall until he found the precious 'spliff', and he put it in his pocket. Now he needed somewhere quiet to go and smoke it.

Jumping back on his bike, he rode down the lanes to a rocky cove just along the coast. He felt the sweat from the exertion of pedalling dripping down his back. He wiped his brow with his sleeve, trembling a little with excitement. He was on a mission and felt exhilarated at the prospect of doing something new.

The sea was gently rolling into the shore. It was calm and there was a quiet stillness to the waters. Ben ambled over the rocks, his rucksack slung over his shoulder. In it there was a telescopic fishing rod, reel and a small box of tackle. He climbed further, along the rocks, which were made slippery from the long strands of kelp left behind from high tide. He skipped over the rock pools, occasionally missing his foothold and soaking his well-worn trainers and socks.

Eventually, after some deliberation he found the perfect spot, a hidey hole in a hummock of tall grasses. He edged himself into it and looked out to sea. He could see distant fishing boats casting their lobster pots. Seagulls glided over the blue- green water, skimming the surface with skill and grace.

He assembled his rod, baited his hook, and cast his line. He munched on the few fragments left of his stolen Hobnobs, which tasted delicious. He lay back, content in his labours. With a start he suddenly remembered why he had come here in the first place. He fumbled in the rucksack for the spliff he had retrieved from the wall, trembling in excitement. Without hesitation, he held the grubby spliff to his lips and lit the end. He drew deeply, and a stream of smoke drifted down into his lungs. His body reacted to the onslaught immediately. He coughed, sputtered and almost vomited. His head began to spin and his mind began to drift. He stared down to the sea immediately below, trying to steady his vision.

There seemed to be a strange hue to the water, which began to swirl like a whirlpool. In the midst of the watery spiral there seemed to be a glowing blue shape. It gradually became more distinct, and morphed into something vaguely humanoid. It had a long slender body and its limbs were moving in a kind of balletic dance. Its movements showed grace and precision. He could see it quite clearly, only just below the surface.

As he looked more closely it dawned upon him that the creature's large blue eyes were fixed upon him in a deep penetrating stare. He didn't feel afraid, more that he was connected as never before, mesmerised by its intensity. His vision faltered and he seemed to fall into a darkly spinning vortex. His body began to move along this tunnel lightly, yet accelerating to an incredible speed. He began to feel extreme nausea and dizziness, and momentarily lost vision.

Coming to his senses, he found himself standing on a platform looking out towards a completely alien landscape, like nothing he had ever seen before. He felt the presence of another being, beckoning him to come closer. He felt strongly that something was trying to communicate with him. Incomprehensible images filled his mind and strange sounds filled the air. His vision blackened again, and he felt himself falling into unconsciousness.

# PLANET NEON/QUILLIAM

In Seronia the day began uneventfully, as the rays of the sun filtered gently through the dome, casting shadows amongst the towering buildings of the city. In one of the more affluent apartments, a young Seronian lay in his bunk, immersed in conversation with a device in front of him.

Quilliam belonged to a family who were typically B Faction, the second level in the hierarchy. This was a favourable position and they were well provided for. Family units such as this consisted of a surrogate pair who were responsible for one offspring, who possessed the same biological imprint of the parents but had been conceived in the procreation units. The surrogates took over the responsibility of the offspring as soon as it was deemed viable to do so. Usually, there was a period of nursery where early development could be monitored, but the transfer to the surrogate home was considered imperative for the offspring's emotional well-being.

In this family, the young male had reached the priapic stage, a pubescent period. He was a youngster of a similar age to Ben and he was about to be called to complete his Investiture Profiling. Quilliam was actually far less excited about this event than his surrogates were. As he did most mornings, he lay half asleep in his bunk, linked to his HPI, a perceptual imaging device. He was finding it hard to complete a final mind transfer, involving a programme about the physical aspects of his own planet. He was finding some aspects quite tedious.

He tried to listen attentively to a soft digitised voice which was giving an exposition of the physical geography of his world.

'Planet Neon, diverse and extraordinary. The Domains - Seronia, Calfaria, Tharmenia'

A globe appeared and various images began to fill the room.

It continued. 'The largest colony in the southern region is Seronia, the embodiment of Neonian technology.'

An image of a great city, pulsating with life was projected around him. He could see the gleaming pinnacles of the city skyline. These were encapsulated in an opaque, organic dome. He could also see the aquatic suburbs which lay beneath the majestic blue green waters of the ocean. As the sun shone across the waves, a prism of light lit up their structures. This was an architecture that was in tune with nature, simplistic and elegant.

'What lies beyond the dome?' he asked.

Immediately he experienced the novelty of a completely different landscape, featuring the distant jagged amber peaks of the Ariane mountain range in Tharmenia

'Do you wish to see more?' a soft voice asked.

'Yes ... take me to ... mm... there.' He pointed at a lush violet coloured pasture filled with blue zasmina.

He took a deep breath. He was intoxicated by its exotic aroma. He longed to go out there, beyond the dome and explore untamed wilderness.

He dared himself to ask. 'Show real time, and life beyond.'

'Beyond there is no survival, the dome protects you.'

He then remembered wanting to further his questioning but was disturbed by the dulcet tones of Cora, the virtual assistant that people had come to utilise constantly.

'Are you awake, do you want full immersion this morning?'

Although he felt a heady exhaustion he replied, 'Be there in three pips!'

He alighted from his bunk and headed toward the sanitation pod. As the doors slid open a pool of refreshing mineral enriched emollient water beckoned him. As he immersed his body into the gel-like emulsion he caught sight of himself in the reflective panels. His long angular shape was beginning to show the signs of maturity, which unnerved him slightly. As he emerged from the pool he could not shake off the feeling of apprehension. Cora recognised his reserve.

'Do you need counsel?'

'Maybe later,' he replied absently.

He quickly dressed, for the last time, in the juvenile colours of his academy. Quilliam was tall and striking, with white blond hair and piercing violet eyes. He had a confident demeanour, but also a sensitivity which seemed to draw others to him.

He looked around for Pedan, his guardian, and found him in the tech pod, fiddling with various devices.

Pedan was his biological father. A genial eccentric, he had reached the second level of physical maturity, but still retained a full head of platinum-coloured hair, tied back in a top knot. His face bore a few furrows but still possessed an enduring appeal which people found very personable

He was an SISE (senior innovative scientific engineer). As a high ranking individual he had worked on many prestigious projects, although a shadow lay over his present relationship with the Directive, due to a misdemeanour which had actually been beyond his control. He tried ever since to keep himself removed from further scrutiny as much as possible.

He muttered to himself, 'If I could just connect the retract to diode one mmm ... perhaps the other way round, no, no maybe reverse the magnetic tribens and bring them back into alignment with the manifold ... mmm.'

He turned and saw Quilliam was standing behind him. 'Have you finished your studies?' he asked.

'Yes but I was wondering, WHY can't we ever go beyond the dome. Has anyone ever ventured out?'

'No one could exist beyond!' Pedan quickly changed the subject. 'Let me see, the resonator needs to be in tune with the ...'

Mi, the prima surrogate, entered the room, looking perturbed, as she had overheard the conversation.

'Go outside the dome! What a foolish notion, Quilliam, the Directive forbids it, we could not survive.'

'Surely there could be some way to explore it?' He felt she was being particularly evasive.

She directed her thoughts towards Pedan.

'Does he not understand the history of the Great Catastrophe?'

'Shhh! That mind transfer may have eluded him,' replied Pedan raising an eyebrow. 'We must ensure that his vulnerability is not compromised.'

Mi looked perplexed at that.

'Don't worry, I'll reprogramme the learning cube so that he is well prepared.'

Pedan sighed, as he was already feeling overburdened by his work, which now frustrated rather than rewarded him. He had once had the freedom to pursue his own ambitious projects, but no longer. Circumstances beyond his control had brought about the disapproval of the Directive. This had made life difficult. There were reprisals for anyone who challenged the status quo. He worried that Quilliam's active imagination might get him into trouble too in the future. Mi's slavish devotion to obedience and conformity also irritated him, but he was careful not to show his feelings.

# THE CEREMONY

Today was the day of Quilliam's Investiture Profiling, which was very important to Pedan and Mi. It would be emotionally draining, as they were both anxious as to whether he had completed his studies to the level expected for transfer to the Institute.

Mi, as usual, was immaculately turned out. Dressed in a crisp white tunic which was tightly drawn around her slender shape, she looked very graceful. Her hair, adorned by a silvery blue clip, fell elegantly in coiffured waves down her back. She had borne the years with considerable dignity.

Cora detected the approaching transport, announcing, 'Shuttle to Alpha approaching, ETA five.'

They made their way to the platform outside and boarded the shuttle. The bright lights and the clinical severity of its furnishings had subdued the occupants, who sat motionless, staring ahead and making no eye contact. They sped along the sky rails, bodies moving in unison as the shuttle turned and twisted. Eventually, they came to a halt. Everyone surged forward and the doors opened onto a platform. They had reached the Academy.

'Please mind the doors as you alight, enjoy your day,' uttered the operative as they spilled out onto the entrance platform of the Academy. Pedan murmured, 'Here we are, let's hope all goes well.'

Mi whispered in his ear, 'Oh I hope so, do you think he has concentrated enough during his mind transferences?'

'The next level will be so much more exciting.' He tried to reassure her without giving away his doubts.

As they entered the building they were greeted by a facilitator droid.

'The Directive welcomes our esteemed plenipotentiaries,' it squeaked in an irritating little voice.

Rows of anxious students and their guardians filled an elaborate amphitheatre. The droid ushered them to their seat near a podium where the Mahonic Legislature assembled. The proceedings began with a grandiose techno display which added to the atmosphere of tense anticipation. As the display came to an end amidst appreciative slapping, the facilitator droids ushered the students onto the podium, where they waited to be called. On a raised podium, the august, dignified figure of the don stood up and addressed the assembly.

'Elite Zone One students, the Directive calls upon you to accept the Academy Credits. Our future lies in your hands, thank you for your hard endeavours and determination.'

It was considered a great honour to be in the presence of the don. He was the master of the Academy, who personally presented the awards. One by one, the students filed past him, and collected their designations.

When it came to his turn, Quilliam nervously ascended towards the podium. Pedan recognised the colour of the object the don handed to him.

'Excellent, he's got a trang!'

'What does that lead to?' Mi asked anxiously.

'If he's lucky he'll go onto the MT programme, which will be perfect for him.' Pedan smiled at her.

Mi looked anxious. She hoped that they had prepared him sufficiently. She was worried that he seemed ambivalent to the whole thing.

After the presentation, Quilliam stood quite motionless at the edge of the arena. He needed to gather his thoughts and found himself ambling along an adjacent corridor, at the end of which there was a doorway that led to the edge of the orb. His curiosity got the better of him and he peered through a gap in a shuttered window. He gasped at the scale of the building, which seemed to dwarf the amphitheatre.

Suddenly, he heard a mechanical voice. 'No unauthorised personnel. It is recommended that you return to the safe zone!' Quilliam thought the tone of the android was overly officious.

'Sorry!' But before he could say another word it gently turned him around.

'You are now redirected, we will see you next semester. Enjoy your vacation Quilliam!'

Unperturbed, he ambled back. When he arrived back in the great hall, Mi grabbed hold of his arm in annoyance. 'Where have you been?'

'I just needed to get some air,' he replied dutifully.

'Really, Quilliam, you must follow the rules, especially today.' She looked over and noticed that Pedan was having a. intense discussion with the don.

'The consequences will be catastrophic, you absolutely must complete it soon. Time is of the essence,' he snapped at Pedan

They quickly changed their expressions as Mi and Quilliam approached.

'Ah, yes, we must talk again soon,' barked the don as he turned and left. Mi was aware that Pedan was agitated.

'What was that about? Is everything okay? Quilliam shouldn't have wandered off like that, I hope we haven't been sanctioned!'

'No, no, everything is fine. In fact, Quilliam has done remarkably well.' He didn't want her to get suspicious so he changed the subject. 'Let's enjoy the rest of the day, we have earned it!'

They returned to the arena and after a final speech from the don, the festivities came to an end. The surrogates and their charges bid farewell and were ushered back to their shuttles. Quilliam would return after his long awaited vacation.

In the shuttle Pedan looked anxious but he handed Quilliam a data chip, 'It seems you have earned this!' He smiled.

'Wow! A Star Dome Pass!'

# PLANET EARTH/ A SORRY AFFAIR

Life had not treated Grace well. The fact that she spent most of her days lost in morbid recollections of past events had taken a toll on her. She was a pale shadow of her former self.

Today was much the same as every other day. She made a half-hearted attempt to get out of bed as she heard Ben scrambling down the stairs but then lay back. She had tried hard to cope with the strain of raising Ben and his step brother Jimmy on her own but the stress had drained her. She could manage Ben, but Jimmy seemed to be a world unto himself. He was the baggage that had come along with her relationship with Frank. She now regretted the affair.

The dreadful loneliness she felt after the loss of Yan had made her vulnerable. She realised that she had made a mistake letting Frank into her life.

There had been so many unanswered questions and the devastation was always there in her mind.

She sat on the stool by her dressing table and looked in the mirror. She ran her fingers through her tousled grey curls and pinned them up onto the top of her head. She was still an attractive woman with a perfectly formed face and soulful dark brown eyes, although time and events of her life had taken their toll. She looked wistfully and sighed. She took hold of the pendant which hung around her slender neck. Then her thoughts began to wander. 'How did things become so?' she whispered under her breath.

She looked out across the bay, watching the little fishing boats going back and forth. She looked pensively at the distant horizon and felt a deep sense of sadness.

'Life is just not fair. She felt a wave of anger surge through her body. 'Why did you have to leave me?' A tear ran down her cheek, which she briskly wiped away.

She had promised herself never to forget, but the memories were fading. Then an image crept into her mind, of Yan standing on the deck of the motor cruiser. He looked so real that she reached out as if to touch him.

She went over to the bed and lay down once more. She felt the heavy weight of her head as it sank into the pillow in exhaustion and melancholia. She closed her eyes and began to remember the events of that evening in the Fisherman's Arms all those years ago. Her mind was filled with such intense memories.

Things had gone from bad to worse since Yan's disappearance. Although people had tried in their own way to be kind, it had been difficult for her to respond and overcome her grief in the years following Yan's disappearance.

'Why oh why did I let that happen?' she cried quietly, her mind in turmoil as she remembered the fateful meeting with Frank.

When she was standing in the queue at the local supermarket, she had overheard ...

'There's that poor woman whose husband went missing, drowned off the Emerald Rocks.'

She felt herself freeze and dropped the basket of groceries she was holding. The eggs smashed and some apples rolled away under the counter. She could feel everyone staring at her. With trembling hands and tears rolling down her face she tried to pick everything up.

Frank had been standing behind her and went to her assistance.

'Let me help you, Gracie, don't listen to them.' He tried to comfort her as she began to sob.

'Thank you, it's just so hard.' She looked up and suddenly realised who was speaking.

'Oh! Hello, Bluey!' It was a comfort to see one of her childhood friends. They had been in the same class at school and Frank had caused quite a stir with his ludicrous Halloween costume. The nickname 'Bluey' had stuck with him for quite some time. He suddenly remembered, particularly the teasing, but he saw it was an opportunity to get her to talk to him.

Keen to cheer her along, he replied, 'No one has called me that for years, cheek of you.' He laughed. At least he seemed to be cheering her up. 'Come on, let me take you for a cup of tea.' He took her arm and gently led her out of the shop. They went to a little cafe at the end of the jetty.

'Some things never change,' she said, staring wistfully at the floral curtains and the peeling edges of the strange mural of a mermaid that adorned the cafe wall.

'You can say that again, do you remember when we used to hang around in the corner over there?' He felt happy to be in her company.

'Yes, I remember.' She laughed gently. 'Goodness it was such a long time ago.' She was glad to have someone to talk to. Frank was very obliging and meeting up with him was a great distraction from the constant sense of loss. They sat there and talked for what seemed to be hours.

She reminded him of his pathetic Blue Man costume. 'You really did go overboard on that costume didn't you? Just tell me, Frank, what happened?'

'Aw, that was the worst experience of my life, I used the blue gloss paint in my dad's garage. I didn't realise it wouldn't come off!' he said. 'And my mother tried to scrub it off, my skin was so sore!!' They both laughed.

'Well I bet the Blue Man himself had a giggle that day, do you think those stories were true about the kelpie?'

'Well, there might be something, but one thing is for certain – I won't be painting my face again!'

It was the first time that Grace had laughed for a long time.

Over the next month or two Frank began to hang around more frequently, and was always on hand when she had a problem with the house or car.

'Well he's kind and thoughtful. I could do worse,' she thought to herself.

'Honestly, Gracie, this place needs fixing up, and that car of yours ...' in this way he gradually made himself indispensable.

She gradually found herself spending more time with him, enjoying his company and forgetting her grief at least momentarily. Things then came to a head one night when they were at the Fisherman's Arms.

Her uncle's gaze met Frank's and he blurted out jokingly,

'Isn't it about time you two got it together?'

Frank looked unusually reticent, Grace looked at Frank. Something about his demeanour seemed suddenly attractive. She had always known that he had a soft spot for her but this was the first time that she considered him as a prospective partner. She was so desperately lonely and it was obvious that Frank was completely smitten with her.

It wasn't long before things began to develop further. Frank could not have been happier, particularly after all the heartache he had suffered with Maisie. However, his son Jimmy would be a thorn in his side, because he resented Grace for taking all of Frank's attention. He disliked Ben even more. When he and Frank finally moved in with Grace, he made things as difficult as possible. Ben tried to avoid him as much as he could.

As the weeks turned into months and the months to years it became apparent that this was not a match made in heaven. 'Stop nagging me, I'm going out!' followed by the slam of the door was becoming more and more the norm.

In time, the novelty of being with a man again wore off, and she began to find Frank hard to cope with. He in turn found it difficult to be in her company and became increasingly withdrawn. He sought refuge at the pub and began to spend less and less time at home.

A vicious argument broke out between them on the night that marked the anniversary of Yan's disappearance.

'For God's sake, Gracie, when will you get it into your head that he's gone?!'

'Don't you dare speak about him that way, he's not gone!' she screamed back at him.

'He's dead, wake up, woman, and see the truth!'

'Get out of here, I never ever want to see you again!'

'Fine, I'm gone!' With that he left the house and went back to live with his sister.

Jimmy, however, refused to move. He liked living in the big house and enjoyed getting his own way. In time he grew more tiresome, his moody adolescent tantrums becoming insufferable. He wasn't particularly bright and disliked his step brother Ben. He was a heavily built lad who liked to push his weight around and had a reputation for being a bit of a bully.

Needless to say, Jimmy and Ben were chalk and cheese. They did not get on at all. While Ben was usually studying or daydreaming, Jimmy was always up to some mischief or other. Grace had little control over him and no real relationship, which added to her sadness and despair.

# PLANET NEON/ ETHEREA

Pedan and Mi were delighted that Quilliam had made such good progress. The 'Star Dome' pass they had rewarded him with gave him entry into a racing circuit for 'free boarders'. They felt this might just keep him on track, at least for now.

'Now be careful, we will see you later ... don't be late!'

He grabbed his tech bag and board and set off for the Star Dome.

The Star Dome was one of many games that could be played in the virtual world of 'Etherea'. This zone was where individuals could explore all kinds of experiences. It was used for pleasure, education and exploration. These experiences, although cerebral, demanded extreme endurance. To engage in the games it was necessary to sign into a booth which was dedicated to the game of choice. At the portal, 'gamers' were given a specific length of time in which they could engage in their chosen activity. Quilliam had been awarded one round.

The Directive, unknown to the Seronians, had taken a primary role in the development of all the virtual activities of Etherea. Ever since it had integrated the minds of Gathine and Tostare into its consciousness it had developed a thirst for more individuality. It wanted to expand its own awareness, and to achieve this, it had surreptitiously begun to absorb individuals into its matrix.

The gaming experience was so compulsive that frequent users became obsessed and lost themselves completely in this world. It was for some a narcotic. As their dependency grew they found all manner of ways to bypass protocols so that they could then spend prolonged periods in this new realm. Ultimately, they became irretrievably immersed. To engage in the experience it was necessary to be connected to the transcranial 'doppler'. This was a synaptic link which was attached to an implant in the brain. If it was operating correctly, the function would cease after a limited period of time. However, some gamers had learned to override this function in order to increase their 'in' time. This was very dangerous and often resulted in their physical bodies becoming severely dehydrated.

It was often impossible to resuscitate those who had over indulged, as the worst cases drifted into a comatose state, kept alive through the intervention of machines and still connected to the Directive's virtual world. These unfortunate users lost their real existence permanently and became figures of the Ethereal world. They were known as 'Ethereas'.

Through this process, the Directive was enlisting recruits. Over time, it assimilated many individuals. Once inside the matrix they had to be monitored, as they still thought like Seronians, and could not be allowed to wander freely within the system. A controller was created to supervise them. If they failed to comply, a shutdown was instigated and their roles terminated. This resulted in their physical death as well. Very few Ethereans were aware that the

Directive had the power to terminate lives, and none of them had any idea how it could be controlled. Once locked into the matrix, Ethereans were assigned to various roles, one of the most common being attendants to the games. They would assist the players and ensure their satisfaction and pleasure. The Star Dome was particularly popular.

Quilliam delighted in the challenges. Here he had been able to hone his race boarding skills. He waited for the shuttle with high excitement, and on his arrival prepared for the games at one of the star port's docking areas, inspecting his board carefully. It could skim the waves of the virtual 'hydra' at unparalleled speed, changing shape and form according to both velocity and nature of the environment it encountered. Sometimes it would dive at supersonic speed, other times it would shoot up in almost impossible trajectories. The skill was to remain upon it.

On his virtual arrival a challenger droid inspected his board. Quilliam was slightly worried as he had adjusted the stabilising wings beyond safety parameters to give him more speed. Fortunately, they let him through.

Then he heard a voice. An Etherean entered the gaming space.

'Hydro board and Sephora ... activating protective gel ... you have thirty ions to complete the tenth quadrant challenge.'

Feeling slightly nervous, he stood with the other free boarders on the start line. The skill was to negotiate each elevation without putting a foot down or falling off. The first to reach nine would get an opportunity to ride a quadrant thirteen triboard. Out of nowhere a voice sounded in his head. 'Beat you to zero one.'

He turned his gaze and recognised that there was a Calfarian telepath in the next lane.

'We'll see about that,' he smiled.

Marli was a Calfarian from Zone 2. She looked resplendent in the silver and ruby clothing that hugged her taut and angular physique. She carefully piled her long amber hair into her helmet and attached the safety guards.

A siren rang out followed by, 'Get into your positions ... Go!'

They then sped off on their star boards. As they approached the first bends, Marli seemed to misjudge the distance between them and their boards and they collided. They rolled over and over and eventually came to land. Quilliam saw Marli lying on the ground and went to her assistance. As he approached she was beginning to recover from the fall.

'Are you okay?' he asked anxiously

'I'm fine, I'm so sorry, I've ruined your chance for the triboard.'

'No problem,' he replied, although he was a little bit disappointed.

Within minutes an Etherean arrived to assist him, however, there was something unusual about it. They usually appeared as uniformed servers, who simply performed their function and then disappeared.

He noticed it had an unusual insignia on the lapels of its uniform. It was an image of a Tharmenian unicorn. Quilliam would later learn that it was a member of a rebel group within the Etherean world.

A subgroup of Ethereans had connected to Gathine and Tostare, the first captives of the Directive. They had constructed a secret sanctuary within the Directive itself, from which they could make contact with some of the lost players who had become Ethereans. The symbol on the insignia was that of a Rarwhal, a mythical Tharmenian creature, and its name was used as a password for all communications.

Quilliam looked across at Marli, who was holding her arm in some discomfort, while the 'regular' Etherean was giving assistance

Then the rebel Etherean turned to him and whispered, 'You will be going on a long and dangerous journey. We will be with you, you need not fear.'

It clenched a fist to its chest and then disappeared.

'That was more than odd,' Quilliam thought. No Etherean had ever behaved like that. It unnerved him and he felt a strange dissociation.

Another voice cut across and could be heard saying, 'Returning user to portal.'

Marli had been taken out of the game. She would be transported to the edge of the zone, where she would sign out from the VR and return to her home in the underwater sphere.

Quilliam glanced across at her, smiling in embarrassed confusion. Marli noticed his Beta Faction designation badge, and realised their conversation may have compromised him. Despite this, she had felt such a powerful connection to him that she dared herself to message him telepathically

'Don't worry, I'll contact you,' she flashed to him as she left.

# MARLI

The situation between Calfaria and Seronia had become more and more complex. An agreement had been reached whereby the Seronians managed to lease back the various acquired 'levels' as long as the Calfarians agreed to continue supplying the kelp. This would always be contentious as the Calfarians resented their territory being encroached upon. However, there were some incentives for them to comply.

Marli was a Zone 2 Calfarian, from an underwater realm, categorised as Z Nexus. This meant that she was allowed access into the gaming area of the Star Dome. Z Nexuses were considered to be high functioning beings with unusual talents which impressed the Seronians. Marli was exceptional, even within this group. She had prodigious aquatic skills and had trained as an instructor for the youth programme.

The Seronians offered a variety of educational programmes which they hoped would help them to integrate with one another. The Calfarians desired peaceful co-existence and agreed to cooperate. One of these programmes was the Nascent Natation Programme. Young Calfarian children could enrol on this to improve their aqua abilities. This proved to be a very popular pursuit.

Mi's reaction when she discovered that Quilliam had been socialising with a Calfarian, even one of Marli's designation, was one of typical Seronian haughtiness.

Following him into his room, she called, 'Let's just call it a chance encounter and be done with it,' and then continued, 'You must understand that this is the way it must be. The stability of the zones cannot be compromised.'

Pedan entered the room.

'Perhaps the Directive could begin to change,' he said.

She glanced at him in frustration, refusing to countenance his suggestion.

'We can discuss this at another time, I'm late,' she snapped as she swept out of the room.

'There's so much I don't understand,' said Quilliam.

'All in good time,' said Pedan. He smiled at his youthful innocence and ambled off to fiddle with a diode retractor. Quilliam returned to his bunk.

As he began to fall asleep that night he was aware of a TP, and although it disturbed him, he relished the communication.

'It's you isn't it? What's your name?'

'Marli,' she replied, and they talked silently into the night.

The vacation passed all too quickly and the day came for him to take his place at the Institute. It was a calm, bright morning. 'Have you got everything?' said Mi anxiously.

Cora interrupted, 'All complete and ready.'

'Don't forget to initialise!' Pedan chipped in completely unnecessarily, not really knowing what to say.

Quilliam glanced back as he waited for the shuttle. He was excited but also sad to be leaving the home he had known for so long.

The shuttle arrived promptly and in no time at all he was at the entrance to the Institute. There were several hundred other internees disembarking. He was led to the welcoming hall by a service droid.

A VERA droid was assigned to him. He remembered to initialise it.

'Q one delta X, authorise,' he intoned, then waited until he heard the reply.

'Authorisation complete, welcome Quilliam!'

VERA would now accompany him wherever he went. It was about the size of a football. Its technology was complex. Its main function was that of a spherical floating droid, but if necessary it could transform. The bio imprint of Quilliam had activated its intel which was now completely focussed on offering assistance at all times.

For the young Seronian it was a long day and he was very weary by the end of it. The whole morning had been dedicated to understanding the concept of synapse links followed by a long discourse on protocols within the Directive. Quilliam was curious about the Directive's prime function.

VERA was quick to enlighten him, 'The Directive maintains our complex social order.'

It seemed to get agitated when he asked, 'Why?'

'Without social order the consequences would be turmoil and ultimately conflict.'

He then asked, 'How do you know this?'

VERA replied, 'I refer to the records of the Ancients and the time of the Great Change.'

'What was the Great Change?' asked Quilliam.

'All will be clear when you experience the J planet, but

we will guide you, you will understand.'

Quilliam was a little unnerved by this, but he was resigned to learning more about the J planets. He appreciated the fact that it would be a privilege to have a close encounter from the unique platform of another world, although it was all a little overwhelming.

He appreciated the advantages of living at the Institute. He would be able to please his parents that he was there, and yet spared their disapproval of any aspects of his behaviour, especially where Marli was concerned. VERA, however, would be monitoring his every move. His first challenge would be to learn how to distract it.

That evening the little droid seemed to be wherever he went, keeping up a constant chatter which had begun to irritate him.

'My primordial functions are to act as a friend and console. Would you like to have a game?'

'Er, no,' was Quilliam's reply.

`Would you like to listen to the latest music?' it asked, filling the room with inaudible sounds.

'No, VERA, go and reboot or something!'

Sulkily it slid into a corner and began a system check.

Quilliam seized the opportunity to TP Marli. 'Are you there?'

There was a momentary silence, then a reply. 'Yes, how's your day?'

'Tedious, I'm followed around by an annoying little droid.'

'Ha, it serves you right for being an annoying little Seronian!'

'That's not fair, maybe you're just a watery nymph, a

figment of my imagination.'

'Next time I see you this figment will knock your block off!' she quipped. They continued teasing one another into the night, although they were both aware of strong affection developing for one another.

The next day the programme began in earnest. There were, however, periodic recesses and leisure activities, so life was not too onerous. He settled into the routines.

Time passed in this way for several weeks, until one particular day when

VERA suddenly became very agitated, making less and less sense, it started to go into lockdown. Another droid appeared which seemed to be far less empathic.

'Re-evaluation for Quilliam. Assignment to DCT.' (Direct communicative transfer.)

As it was very unusual for internees to be reassigned so quickly. Quilliam grew agitated. He felt that he must have done something very wrong in order to initiate such a drastic measure. Wondering whether it may have been due to his relationship with Marli, he decided to initiate a TP.

Marli responded immediately, 'What's wrong Q?' she asked.

'They are going to re-evaluate me!'

'Really, is that usual? You don't seem to have been there long, maybe you just miss me, eh?'

'I'm not joking, this is serious. Doesn't feel right, maybe they know about us, gotta go. I can hear them coming for me!'

Quilliam had indeed been under suspicion since he had entered the orb on the day of his investiture. Also his strange behaviour and communications with Marli hadn't gone unnoticed. He could not have known the consequences of these actions.

As the TP concluded, she felt a certain pang of anxiety, and resolved to investigate the situation as soon as he had finished her shift. She was employed at the aqua, and looked radiant in her submesentric colours, which denoted her as a fifth-level aqua trainer. She was teaching a young group of level 1 how to gill breath. They stood nervously in their metallic violet suits waiting for her instructions. She demonstrated how to enter the aqua and submerge gradually down to the first overhang.

The little group was full of excitement. They were hopping from foot to foot eager to get into the water.

'Ok, ok sorry to keep my little frylings waiting!' And with no further preamble

Marli dived into the aqua. As soon as she broke the surface an array of bubbles surrounded her. Her body seemed to twist in a balletic corkscrew, causing a pattern of waves to spiral around her in a kaleidoscope of iridescent colours.

'Wow!' the group gasped as one in delight.

'Right, it's your turn, I want you to take a deep breath and dive. When you are under, open your gills. Ready?'

The group lined up on the edge and, one by one, dived into the aqua. They disappeared into the depths, then suddenly turned and began to shoot upwards. The water began to boil with bubbles as their delighted little heads broke the surface.

Marli was pleased with their confidence and enthusiasm.

'Okay, let's try that again; off you go!'

Again they plunged in, they excitedly wriggled and

darted beneath the first level where they hung still like little fish.

Suddenly, Marli caught sight of one individual sitting on the edge of the aqua, looking lost and upset.

Marli swam over to investigate.

'It's Shira, isn't it? What's the matter?'

'I'm scared, I don't think I can do it,' she said, wiping a tear from her eye.

'Of course you can, you just need a little practice. Would you like to play a game with me?'

Shira looked up and thought that might be more fun.

'You will be fine, let's just play tag. Follow me!'

With a splash both were in the water. The child still felt unsure and clung onto Marli as she rolled over and over in the water.

'See if you can catch me?' said Marli.

Shira let go and swam behind Marli, who let her catch her over and over until they rolled over in the aqua, laughing. Gradually, Shira's confidence began to grow. Marli swam alongside her and leaned close. 'Just close your eyes and breath,' she whispered. Then she dived deeply into the aqua, taking the child with her. As she gracefully descended, her angular body enveloped the child, who finally began to breathe steadily through her gills. Marli then released her as she swam up to the surface like a wriggling seal. She watched as she played fearlessly in the waves diving and surfacing.

Quilliam's TP had alarmed her. She sensed something was wrong. She gathered her troupe together and returned them to their anxiously waiting parents.

One shouted across to her, 'Did she do it?'

'Yes, like an angel fish, a natural!' She smiled as the parent beamed with pride. As soon as the parents and children had left, Marli began to worry about how she could help her Seronian friend.

Quilliam, in the meantime, was unceremoniously marched to the sphere, with no explanation given, followed by the droids. He felt a sense of unease when he entered the huge chamber. He was led to a capsule, where he was seated in a cocoon-like chair, and an array of sensors and wires attached to him.

His mind went blank. He desperately tried to focus but was overwhelmed. He could feel his heart beating, although he had no control of his body. He felt as though he was weightless and floating in something that was not aqua. Then he began to feel as if he was spiralling down a vortex. His body seemed to be transformed, almost fluid. Images flashed incomprehensibly past his vision. At one point he seemed to open his eyes and looked up to a completely unfamiliar landscape. He tried to reach out with his hand, and in that moment, he made contact. Just for a second he felt that something was looking back at him from that landscape. He felt a chill go up and down his spine. He couldn't comprehend what was happening to him. He tried in vain to call out, but no sound came. It was too much for him. In a flash it was over, and all went blank.

In the DCT chamber there was a great deal of consternation. A digital display dropped down from the ceiling above Quilliam's unit. The capsule in which he lay began to display function failures. VERA moved various symbols around on the screen but seemed to be unable to control what was occurring, so it summoned assistance from the medical droids. They attached themselves to the capsule and began emergency procedures.

'Monitoring zeta waves, initiate system CX one, assist immediately.'

'Life support system activated.'

Analyse contaminant.'

Despite their efforts, Quilliam could not be revived. An emergency transfer was made from the sphere to the orb where he was placed in an intensive support unit.

'Dionic mind transference error, system closure,' intoned one of the drones.

'Toxic level ... beta,' said the medic in attendance.

'Exposure to a viral mind infection, initiate complete isolation.'

At that moment the superiors were summoned, in consultation with the Mahon.

Pedan and Mi were summoned to the orb, where they were met by the assembled group.

'Why the sphere?' Mi asked Pedan.

'I'm not sure, perhaps a precaution,' he said trying to comfort her

At that moment Cora said, 'Please, do not be alarmed, this is a standard procedure.'

They were led to the decontamination unit. From the viewing tower they could see Quilliam was lying prone in the capsule.

'No, no! this can't be! What's happening to him?' Mi cried out in desperation.

Pedan became very concerned. Mi fixed upon him a penetrating stare. 'I hope you reprogrammed the learning cube, otherwise ...'

He tried to avoid her gaze. Pedan realised that he had been too preoccupied at the time, and that it had slipped his mind.

Mi read the expression on his face.

'Oh no! How is he going to cope? He's not prepared for a primal experience.'

# PLANET EARTH – PORT LAR

Ben could not understand how he found himself back in the village. He was aware that he had had a very strange experience and felt confused. He had somehow in this 'stoned' state managed to collect himself together and was walking down the main road of the village. He looked for his rucksack, but it wasn't on his back and his beloved bike was nowhere to be seen.

'What the?' Then to his horror he could see an angry shape heading towards him. It was his brother Jimmy.

'Ben you f ... git, where the f ... have you been?' Jimmy was red in the face. 'You are gonna really get it this time, wait till I get hold of you. Mum is going crazy!'

Ben felt irritated by him calling Grace his mum and was alarmed by all the fuss. Apparently, he had been gone all night. His mother had rung the police. Everyone had been shocked by his sudden disappearance.

Fortunately for Ben, 'Pirate J', who had been the last person to see him, was standing at the side of the road trying to unsuccessfully kick start his beloved 'Triumph'. As Ben wandered towards him he grabbed hold of him

'Bloody hell, Ben, you gave us all a fright, come on I'll take you home, son.'

Ben clambered into Pirate J's sidecar. The engine of this

unwieldy contraption started and he could feel the motion of the vehicle move him along the road. He sat very still, breathing very deeply and shaking.

Eventually they reached the house. His mother was standing on the front step, she looked at Ben with horror.

'Oh my God!'

At that point Ben collapsed.

Ben woke up in a small cubicle in the local A & E. His mother was standing beside the bed. 'Pirate J' had his arm around her (this was an opportunity he couldn't miss). His brother was leaning against the wall.

'You nicked my bloody Hobnobs, you little brat,' were the only comforting words he could summon up.

Ben was strangely pleased to see his brother. For some reason he had lost his fear of him. He stared up at his mother, who was stroking his head.

'Mum! It was all so weird ...'

She interrupted him gently, 'We'll talk about it when we get home.' She knew that she had seen that look before.

Back at the house, Ben slowly began to recover from his experience, although, something inside seemed to have changed. He felt different on a level that he could not explain. His mother seemed strangely attentive and seemed to smile at him at every opportunity. A photograph of his dad had reappeared and had been given pride of place on the mantelpiece.

She began to talk about his dad, saying how accomplished he was, how he had been a researcher for the Institute of Physical Science. She talked about his many research expeditions. She mentioned his special project. It had crossed her mind that this experience of Ben's now could be a clue as to what had happened to him.

Unfortunately, Ben was unable to give her any answers. All he could remember were the blue eyes of the creature in the water and that he felt a connection with it. He swore to himself never to smoke any of that weed again.

Ben's experiences hadn't gone unnoticed. Returning from school a couple of weeks later, Tooley was waiting for him at the bus shelter.

'Right, you little fecker, where did you get the scag from?'

'I got it from the wall, get off me, you git!' he said, shoving Tooley into the road.

'Nah you didn't, that was a bit of an oxo cube, I wuz just messin with you all. Do you think I'd waste my real gear on scabs like you?'

So typical of Tooley, Ben thought. Then it dawned on him. If it wasn't the spliff that had affected him, then what had really happened?

Tooley was now beginning to feel that Ben needed to be put down a peg or two. He grabbed Ben by the collar and pulled, leaning his head back in preparation to headbutt him. Ben began to feel very detached from what was happening and strangely calm. His body became rigid as he stared up into Tooley's eyes. At that moment, Tooley froze, let go of him and began to breathe rapidly. His head drooped and his whole body started to twitch. Blood began to drip from his ears, mouth and nostrils and he collapsed to the floor.

At that moment Robbie ran up towards Ben.

'What've you done to Tooley?'

Ben suddenly came to his senses and looked at his

friend. He had no idea about what had just happened

'I ... I ... dunno,' he stuttered as he spoke.

Tooley regained consciousness almost immediately He wiped the blood from his nose, and staggered off, too shocked and dazed to say anything.

Ben was both agitated and confused. He knew that he would have to face Tooley again sometime. He would need to be on his guard.

The news that Ben had 'faced off' Tooley spread through the village like wildfire. It was going to be difficult to explain what he had done. Something inexplicable was running in his veins. He found himself wandering along the rocky cliffs again, staring across at the horizon. He felt a connection with something or somebody that had never been there before. His mind was being bombarded. It was exhausting but exhilarating at the same time. He hoped that he could find a way to understand it all.

Eventually, he found his way home and ran to the sanctity of his bedroom. He lay on his bed and drifted into a strange dream. Ben awoke with his brother Jimmy standing over him.

'Tooley is after you big time!' he said menacingly.

'I ... I don't know what you are talking about,' he said, trying to ignore him.

'You need to come with me,' Jimmy replied

Ben felt compromised. He sensed Jimmy was up to something but, against his better judgement, he followed him to his beaten up old Nissan that was parked at the back of the house. He drove in his usual lunatic manner, speeding along the narrow winding lanes muttering to himself all the while.

Finally, they arrived at an industrial park and stopped outside a scruffy looking building which looked like some sort of engineering works. Two large up and over doors were hanging off their hinges, creaking in the wind. Behind them were containers and boxes that had been discarded many years ago. Water dripped off rusting pipes and chains swung eerily from the ceiling. Huddled in a corner were a group of misfit looking men. They seemed to be weighing various packages and furtively wrapping them.

Ben's brother approached them and then turned to his brother, saying, 'He's the one that beat up Tooley!'

Ben felt betrayed, how could his brother do this to him?

A very tough looking character marched up to Ben carrying a package in one hand. With the other, he grabbed hold of his jacket and faced up to him. Ben could smell something weird in his breath and tried not to look into his cold, mean looking face.

'Right, got a job for you, take this stuff to Tooley, rough him up a bit, and tell him I want a return by next Friday or else!'

Ben held the package tightly and put it in his jacket pocket. They were then ushered out of the building and without looking back, they got back into the car.

Ben sat quietly in the passenger seat. He was still feeling angry and upset. His brother didn't seem to acknowledge him, he just put his foot on the accelerator, the engine roared noisily and they were off.

Ben cried, 'Stop the car, I'm feeling sick.'

Jimmy just drove faster still, shouting, 'Let's just get the job done and then we can go home!' But before he could finish his sentence the car sped off the road and landed in a ditch.

Ben's brother was thrown through the windscreen and landed, crumpled and bloodied, on the road.

Ben leaped out of the car and ran through the muddy field as fast as he could. He ran towards what looked like an old stone shack. He groped his way along the ground and simply lay flat out inside it, staring wildly. He couldn't feel his body, his mind was detached, and he felt himself drifting.

The accident had been witnessed by a cyclist who had seen the car violently swerve off the road into the hedge. Jimmy had sustained major injuries and was soon taken off to the local A&E. The witness had seen someone leave the vehicle and take off into the fields. There was a search made of the area but no one was found.

Ben awoke in his bed. He had no idea how he returned. He was in his pyjamas as normal.

His mother called up to him, 'Ben, get dressed, you will have to go to school later today. Jimmy has been involved in a terrible accident, we've got to go to the hospital, and the police say ...'

She couldn't quite finish her sentence; she was so distressed. Ben got up and dressed. A policewoman escorted them out of the house and into a car which took them to the hospital.

As they stood in the hospital corridor a policewoman took them on one side saying,

'Are you aware that your son was dealing drugs?'

'What! No he wouldn't!' Grace let the words roll off her tongue, although she knew that for some time Jimmy had been out of control.

'And we think there was something suspicious about

this accident. There is a report that someone else was in the car.'

Ben felt his heart thundering in his chest, and then the news came. A doctor in a white coat with a sombre face said, 'I'm very, very sorry. We did everything we could to try to resuscitate him, but Jimmy has unfortunately died from his injuries.'

Ben's mother turned to Ben, looked pale and began to sob. 'How am I going to tell Frank? He will never forgive me for this.' As she held him tightly, he could feel her wet tears in his hair. The police officer looked at them and said, 'We'll get to the bottom of this.'

The case was referred to a criminal investigation unit as Jimmy had been found to be in possession of a quantity of Class A drugs at the time of the accident. There was also the witness account of seeing another person fleeing the scene.

At the house Ben searched through his jacket for the packet he was supposed to deliver to Tooley. He opened it and inside there were bags of powder, pills and a large lump of resin.

He realised that this must be the 'Scag' that Tooley had mentioned. He wasn't sure what to do with it. He looked around his room and, finding an old jigsaw box, he flung all the pieces into the bin and put the gear in it, then stuffed it under his old pine wardrobe under his discarded socks and underpants.

Preparations for Jimmy's funeral were being made. This would take place in the village church. Jimmy's dad, Frank, had appeared and was pacing around the lounge. Other, more distant relatives sat awkwardly on the couch. Frank's sister, Ruth, put her arm around him and said, 'So sorry for your loss, Frank. Jimmy was a wonderful boy.'

Frank just stared out the window, his face contorted with grief and anger.

Ben's mother had retreated to her bedroom. She couldn't face the assembled entourage.

Eventually, Mr Townsend, the funeral director, appeared at the house. The coffin was placed in the hearse and they followed in black limousines. After the funeral service, people from the village assembled around the gates to show their respect. As they passed by, Ben noticed Tooley. He had a vengeful look on his face. As their eyes met, Tooley stuck up his finger and mouthed, 'You're gonna get it this time!'

# PLANET NEON – SERONIA

Despite the best efforts of medical experts, Quilliam was not responding to the mind cleanse, and the prognosis was not good. Pedan and Mi watched over him anxiously day and night.

Pedan requested an interview with those in charge. The clinical director spoke first. 'It is possible that mind dysfunction was induced by some kind of quantum exposure.'

The senior scientific officer then interjected, 'To eradicate the exposure effects, we need to separate the contaminants.'

'How can this be done?' Pedan looked anxious.

The clinical director said, 'We have to consider using the quantum probe itself,' at which the senior looked nervous.

'But isn't it still in the experimental stage?' Pedan was shocked by their suggestion.

# PLANET EARTH/ BEN

After the funeral they returned to the house. Ben retreated to his bedroom, exhausted and drained. A few people from the village had turned up to pay their respects, Tooley included. He sidled up to Grace, saying, 'Sorry for your loss. He was a good mate Jimmy. We were close, me and him. I don't suppose I could have a word with Ben?'

'Yes, by all means, Tooley. Ben's very upset, you will find him upstairs in his bedroom. Might do him good to have a chat with someone.'

'Right, yes, I'll have a chat with him.' He briskly marched past her and up the stairs, looking into each bedroom for Ben. Finally, he found him, he shoved the door open with such a force that Ben was startled

'Right you little brat, where's the scag!'

'Dunno what you are talking about.'

Tooley searched around the room, kicking and throwing things aside. Finally, he ransacked the wardrobe and started pulling things from underneath it. The little jigsaw box tumbled out and the contents spilled onto the floor. Tooley scooped it all up and shoved it into his pockets.

'Right, that's our business over!' At that he scurried down the stairs and left the house as fast as he could.

Ben finally pulled his thoughts together. He was glad

that the gear was gone. Lying on his bed exhausted and sleepy, surreal images began to drift through his mind. Gradually he dozed off.

The next day, the phone rang and Ben answered it.

'Hello, my name is Detective Simon O'Reilly. Could I have a word with your mother?'

Ben, feeling tired and nauseous, didn't want to think what the call might be about.

'Mum, phone, it's that detective bloke.'

He passed the phone to his mother, remembering to press the speakerphone button so that he could hear the conversation.

'Oh, hello there. Is there any more news?'

'I'm just calling to say that we think we know who the other person was in the car with Jimmy.'

She looked at Ben, who was going quite pale. He could feel his heart beating in his chest.

'Oh goodness! Who was it?'

'We think it was the Toole boy. We picked him up in the village last night, just as he was attempting to deal the same types of drugs that were in the traces we found in the car. We have him in the cells now. We'll let you know more once we have questioned him further.'

Ben felt both scared and relieved. It seemed that Tooley's stupidity and greed had played into his hands. Tooley, under the pressure of questioning, gave all the names of the Christchurch drug gang to the detective. During the process, he also tried to implicate Ben. Ben was taken to the police station as a routine procedure and interviewed. Detective O'Reilly took Ben on one side and said, 'Ben, you may well be an innocent bystander in all this, but I've got a funny feeling about it all. Just be thankful that, until further evidence surfaces, the case is closed.'

# PLANET NEON – SERONIA

Pedan had been summoned to an audience with the Mahon. He found this irksome, as he could not tolerate much more interrogation about the progress of the 'probe'.

He was led into the Oralia chamber. The Mahon was standing in a viewing gallery looking out across the city with a stern expression on his face. He waved to the landscape behind him and cried, 'The finest embodiment of Neon technology!'

Pedan just nodded, as he had more important issues on his mind, but the Mahon began, 'There are going to be difficult times ahead.'

The Mahon was looking straight at him, which was unusual.

He dismissed the other superiors and led Pedan to the command control area.

The Mahon became ill at ease and looked distressed. 'I will come straight to the point. The great dome is suffering a sickness. A virus has infiltrated the Rosanthrocae compound that constitutes the dome's iosphere. Look there!' He pointed to an area of the dome which looked almost opaque.

'But surely the Directive could synthesise an antigen to neutralise it?'

'Unfortunately we have been unable to find an organic compound which matches the characteristics we need exactly.'

'Surely an artificial compound could be replicated?'

The Mahon looked irritated. 'We have already tried every possibility. Each time we identify a suitable candidate there's an instability.' He sighed

'We don't understand why something is compromising every effort we make. It's as if there is an inbuilt mechanism defeating us.' He turned to Pedan. 'Perhaps this is our final demise'

'Why are you telling me? How can I—' Before he could finish his sentence the Mahon turned to him.

'The Supreme Council and the Directive are considering all options, it has been suggested that one possible strategy would be to re-instigate the V programme.'

'The V programme was suspended years ago,' cried Pedan, taken aback. 'But,' Pedan paused to think, 'what of the ethics?'

'Indeed, yes, the V programme was technically compromised.'

'If I remember, it wasn't just compromised, it failed!'

'Yes, yes, but we have been re-evaluating and this really is the time to reconsider. I have already made the arrangements. The droids will assist you.'

'What arrangements? Why was I not consulted?' He then turned to the Mahon, his heart racing, but before he could say anything more, the great leader had swept out of the room and was gone.

The V programme was a research project, initiated by Pedan many years ago. Advances had been made in processes which enabled the conscious mind to be separated from its host and directed towards distant locations. Through the use of quantum tunnelling, research probes had transferred awareness to places far across the universe. Further than that, it became possible to transfer material in either direction via the same route. During one such expedition, researchers had identified intelligent life in a system many light years away on a planet known as Earth. Releasing the mind from its host in this manner was, however, a dangerous procedure. The preliminary trials had demonstrated that the inhabitants of this planet had not been able to physically withstand the transfer. It was thus deemed unethical to continue with the research. They did not wish their probes to cause harm to life. It caused them great distress to learn of the fate of one of the experimental subjects, an Earth creature known as Yan.

Yan accidentally encountered the probe when he had fallen overboard during the night of the storm. In order to be as inconspicuous as possible, the probe's interface was programmed to mimic the shape of any life forms that it encountered. Confronted with a human it began to assume that shape. Consequently Yan saw a watery representation of himself, but in the process something was also planted into his subconscious. This subliminal reprogramming of his brain through his encounter with quantum energies was profound.

The encounter had haunted Yan. When he was sleeping he would start muttering in an unknown language. Grace had on many occasions found him in the study drawing and doing strange calculations. She had accepted his behaviours as harmless eccentricities.

For reasons that he could never explain he was deeply

preoccupied with the Emerald Rocks. He was constantly searching the area for something, although he had no clear idea of what it was. He found himself collecting all manner of gastropods and crustaceans.

There was one incident which seemed to be quite unusual. With Grace at the helm of the dinghy they had drifted over to the Rocks. It was a calm day, the sea gently lapping against the shore. They had moored at the jetty and were busily setting up instruments. Yan decided he would begin the day by collecting crustacea from beneath the water line in the cave. He told Grace he would only be there for about twenty minutes but ended up being gone for at least two hours. When he finally appeared he was highly animated. 'Grace, Grace I think I have found it!'

'You didn't tell me what you were looking for,' she said in puzzlement.

'You idiotic woman, this is what I have been searching for all this time!'

'Excuse me, don't be rude to me, and what do you mean?'

He fumbled in haste as he opened a container and said, 'This has got to be kept safe. Put it in the flask and mark it 'Rosanthropod'.'

'What do you mean? How safe does it have to be?'

'As safe as humanly possible!'

He handed it to her and she secured it in the flask. Granted, it was a strangely shaped mollusc, but she couldn't see what was so special about it. Yan seemed so distant and irritable with her that she was deeply upset. However, no sooner had they pushed the boat away from the jetty when he seemed to change back to being the person she knew and loved.

# PLANET EARTH – THE DEMISE

It was a tragedy that Ben had lost his father, but Grace had now lost both her soulmate and her stepson. Nothing seemed to add up. She couldn't understand why this was all happening to her. All she could do was to try to ensure that Ben would emerge from all of this into a better future.

A meeting had been arranged at Ben's school, as teachers had noticed that he was looking very disturbed by recent events. The head was sitting at his desk trying to offer words of encouragement. Mr Bates was also there, as he had expressed an interest in Ben's welfare.

'Well, Ericson, umm, Ben. I am very sorry to hear about your brother, you can rest assured that we will be here to help hmm if ...' he turned to Mr Bates for support. 'Yes, umm my colleague here will be your tutor next year and am sure he will be able to offer assistance, umm, should you require it.'

He glanced towards Mr Bates, who interjected, 'Yes, Ben my boy,' and was about to continue when the head cut him off abruptly, saying, 'Back to your tutor group then, and ah well yes!'

He ushered them out of his room, pleased that the meeting had gone well, although perhaps a little awkward.

Grace smiled wanly, disappointed at the lack of sincerity

the head had displayed.

'You'll be fine, Ben. Won't he, Mr Bates?' She sensed that Mr Bates was a kind man and that he cared about Ben.

'Yes, yes oh yes, Mrs Ericson, we will do our best, c'mon Ben.'

Grace left Ben with Mr Bates, still worried about his welfare, but powerless to do any more for him.

In the following months, Ben seemed to settle down to his studies again, although he became rather more introverted and moody. He seemed to be constantly preoccupied, uninterested in his friends, and spending more and more time alone. He began to look pale and fragile. For some reason his appetite had changed too. He usually consumed everything in the fridge, but now it was hard to get him to eat anything at all. It was assumed that this was a result of the grief he was experiencing for his brother.

Mr Bates did his best to provide encouragement and support. Ben, like his father, had a natural gift for science and was academically far ahead of the other students.

One day, it so happened that Ben had arrived early for some extra tuition. Mr Bates, keen to set his prodigy to work, ushered him into the preparation area, where students were not usually allowed.

'Right, Ben, we seem to have covered most of the theory, but the practical is an essential element. I think with a little practice you will have no problem with the dissection.'

The lab possessed a strange pungent odour. Jars with all manner of specimens were clustered on the shelves. In the sink a cork mat was soaking in formaldehyde, on the edge was a black bin bag. There seemed to be a heavy shape within it.

Mr Bates, dressed in his stained lab coat was busying himself with various pieces of paper and dissection implements.

'Ah yes, we need to make an incision along the abdomen, pull back the inner lining and pin. Where the dickens have I put the pins?'

Ben sat at the bench and looked up at the shelves.

He was fascinated by the specimens. After a few moments of staring, he began to feel very strangely detached from reality. He became fixated on a lizard that was floating in a large jar. He fixed his gaze on it, and suddenly it seemed as though it twitched. He blinked, and dismissed the event as something he had imagined.

Turning his attention to the black bin bag which Mr Bates was hovering over, he watched him reach inside and retrieve the bulbous body of a large green toad, which he then dropped ungraciously into the sink.

'Right, I'll just give this a little rinse and we'll be ready.'

Ben could feel a sense of revulsion. He began to feel nauseous.

Mr Bates busily placed the amphibian on the cork mat and handed a scalpel to Ben.

'Ok, Ben my boy, the first incision. Just watch for the time being, and then it's your turn.'

Bates was about to cut the abdomen open, when the body of the animal began to twitch.

'What the ...?' he muttered, reaching for a hammer with which to euthanize it.

At that moment  Ben stared deeply at him. Mr Bates shouted 'Oh my God stop!'

Mr Bates put his hands on his ears and began to groan in pain.

'Oh no no no! Please please make it stop!' he cried, then collapsed to the floor in a dead faint.

Ben was standing motionless, looking vacant and dazed when the lab technician came running in, crying, 'Oh my God, he must have had a stroke. Ben, don't just stand there! Go get help!'

In minutes there were several staff huddled around Mr Bates. The technician was trying desperately to resuscitate him. An ambulance was called.

Ben was escorted to the staff room, seemingly in a state of shock. His mother was called to take him home. When she arrived she led him to her car. As they drove along the winding road back to the house she remarked, 'What's that croaking noise, Ben?' When she looked across at him she could see he was cradling a live toad.

'Oh goodness, let the poor thing go,' she said, stopping the car by the side of the road and opening the passenger door.

Without any prompting, the toad jumped out and disappeared into the damp greenery of the roadside ditch. Ben could not explain how he came to be cradling the toad. He was aware of feelings of concern for Mr Bates, but also pity for all the lifeless creatures in those bell jars in the lab. These feelings of guilt and compassion for all living things seemed to intensify, to the extent that he could not pass the fishmongers on the quay without feeling grief for the lifeless silvery bodies laid out on display.

Something was changing deep within him and he was unnerved by it, leading him to retreat still further within himself. He would spend many hours poring over books, on both science and esoteric subjects. The world beyond his house seemed increasingly remote to him. He had no time for Robbie and other friends. Sometimes he would cycle down to the cliff top and simply stare out to sea for hours. Grace tried hard to console him, but he seemed to distance himself even from her. She was relieved that he had managed to secure a place at university, thinking that this might just be what he needed. He would be able to start afresh and make new friends

# PLANET EARTH/THE EMPTY NEST

On the morning he was due to leave for university, she held back the tears and quietly stood with him at the door, watching the taxi wind up the hill towards them.

'Make sure you ring or text me often!' she held back a sigh.

'Of course, don't worry.' He waved back at her as the taxi sped off.

Ben looked back toward the cliffs and the sea. He felt a connection that was almost physical, to the green of the cliffs and the blue of the sea. It was a long journey to Strathmoor and the university, but his mood lifted over the hours, in anticipation of the fresh new experiences to come.

The hall he was allocated to was on the top floor of the 'Henry Bliem Wing'. Along the same corridor were four other students. Ahmed was an overseas student, studying biophysics, the same course as Ben. There was Henry, an American studying geography, a Geordie called Kevin, studying computer science, and lastly Jason from the Wirral who was studying engineering.

They all met in the kitchen, which was located at the end of the corridor. Henry seemed assured and confident, which contrasted starkly with Ben's shy reticence. Jason was quite laddish and Kevin seemed affable. Ahmed was obliging and seemed keen to befriend everyone.

Kevin looked to be something of a geek, scruffily dressed and plumpish with curly mousy hair. The fact that he was missing his mum was obvious from the many comments he made about her lovely Sunday dinners. His computer skills were legendary, and he seemed to be always connected to some device or other. Henry was different altogether, being well aware of his good looks he was far more interested in the opposite sex. He was always keen to divulge information about his sexual exploits, which was received with keen interest from the others. Jason was the joker and was always able to invent some kind of slapstick trick which would send them all into fits of laughter.

A recent prank had gone terribly wrong. He had gone to the top of the science building and dropped a huge balloon filled with coloured powders. He had hoped that it would just fall to the ground and create a kaleidoscope of colours on the pavement in front of the foyer. Unfortunately, it burst on an overhang on the way down causing all the colours to splatter against the newly decorated walls of the most prestigious building on the campus. He had managed to disappear before anyone noticed that he was the culprit. Jason was quite overwhelmed by his own stupidity and went into hiding, hardly daring to think what the consequences might be for him if he was discovered. However, other things were afoot that day too. Ben had returned early from his lectures and found Kevin as usual staring at his computer screen.

'You wanna have a go on my PlayStation like, Ben?' he asked in his Geordie twang.

'Yeah, will give it a go,' said Ben.

They perched themselves by the screen and began the game. The graphics were very compelling and Ben found himself drifting further and further inward.

Kevin was at first delighted to be able to share his knowledge and skill in the game but eventually noticed how intense and withdrawn Ben was becoming as he played. After a while, Jason entered the room. 'Move over Ben, let me have a go.'

By this time, Ben's hands were clamped tightly to the controls. His eyes were staring and his body was completely rigid.

Kevin glanced at Jason and gestured that they should try to get him off the computer, gently reaching to try to remove the controller from his hands.

'Get off ... get off me ... you bastards,' he snarled angrily, staring fixedly at the screen.

Kevin reached down and disconnected the power, at which point Ben fell back, staring fixedly at the ceiling as if in a seizure.

'Jesus Christ! What's wrong with him?' shouted Jason.

'Dunno. This is so weird. Think we'd better put him on his bed, maybe it's some sort of fit. You watch him, I'll go get help.'

Jason leaped out of the room and went to get help. Kevin just stared at Ben.

'Oh man, you must have taken some really weird shit!'

After about half an hour Jason returned with a duty officer. By this time, Ben was showing signs of recovery. The duty officer looked up and down, sniffed the air and said, 'Whatever it is you kids have been on, this is your last warning!'

'But, but we haven't,' they cried in unison.

At that moment Ben stood up and walked out of the room, behaving completely as normal.

'I thought you said someone was ill. Come on you lot, stop wasting my time!' he snapped, and marched away down the corridor.

Jason felt angry that he'd been implicated in something he had nothing to do with.

Kevin tried to switch the computer on again, only to discover that it was no longer functioning. Kevin was beside himself. 'Oh shit man, it's completely fried!' he shouted

'Me mam's gonna kill us, that computer cost loads.'

In the following days, Jason and Kevin distanced themselves from Ben, although things did look as though things were back to normal.

Ben, however, found that his theory lectures were becoming rather obvious to him and wished he could spend more time in the research laboratory.

Ahmed found himself very much in Ben's shadow. Ben was racing through every topic, and left him far behind. At first it wasn't a problem, but as the term progressed Ben became less tolerant and rather more solitary. He would return from the lab looking pale and exhausted and would lock himself away in his room.

Ahmed was a little in awe of his intelligence and tried his best to befriend him, but Ben seemed to have little time for him. Just before the term was about to finish he tried once more, plucking up the courage to ask, 'Hey Ben, I would really like to go into the town and sample some of your wonderful English cuisine. Do you fancy it?'

Henry, who had overheard his conversation, replied, 'Fat chance of him doing anything. Tell you what, I'll meet you, Ahmed, meet you about fourish, on Friday.'

Ahmed's face lit up. He really wanted to experience English culture and was tired of trying to get Ben to be his guide..

On Friday at about half past three, Ben was busy mapping the gene code from a sample in the research lab. He lifted the test tube out of the deep freezer and placed it on the stand next to an electron microscope. Ahmed was at the adjacent workstation busily trying to finish up early. He was highly excited at the prospect of going out with Henry and dreamed of the possibility of finally getting to talk to some girls. As he started to take off his lab coat, he passed close to Ben and his sleeve brushed against the sample, knocking onto the floor where it smashed.

Ben became thoroughly agitated and angry.

'You idiot, look what you've done!' he shouted

'Oh I am so, so sorry! Let me help gather it up,' he mumbled in embarrassment, disturbed by the expression of hate on Ben's face.

At that point, Ahmed began to feel quite nauseous. Ben was still staring at him and he felt a power emanating from him. Bood began to trickle from his nose and mouth and he began to gasp for air. Wordlessly, he sank to the ground.

Ben stood rigid, staring blankly into space. At that moment Henry appeared at the door.

'What the fuck! What happened to Ahmed! Quick, get some help!' he shouted.

Several people rushed to the lab and assistance was called. Very soon an ambulance arrived and Ahmed was transported to the local hospital.

Ben seemed deeply preoccupied, fussily attempting to retrieve the sample from the floor. He was sweating and trembling as if in shock. 'Come on, buddy, leave that, let's go!' said Henry.

Silently, Ben grabbed his notes and followed Henry along the corridors back to the hall.

Without a word he rushed into his room and locked the door.

'What the F ...! You're so weird, man,' muttered Henry, who left him alone and went off to the bar.

Ahmed was taken into intensive care. He was sedated and placed in an induced coma and attached to the life support machines. It didn't look good.

When Ben came out of his room there was a distinctly cold atmosphere. He heard Henry say to the others, 'There's something so weird about him. What did he do?'

Ben was completely devastated. Thankfully it was the end of term and he was going home.

# DETECTIVE O'REILLY

It was a cold, drizzly Monday morning. Detective O'Reilly was sitting in his office reading the local gazette. This was his usual routine. He sipped at his coffee and sighed at the prospect of the long week ahead. He reached towards his filing cabinet to put away the folder of a current case. As he put away the folder he accidentally knocked his coffee over another file.

'Shit, Jesus fecking Mary sh ... sh ... shit,' the expletives went on while he pulled it out and wiped the coffee off it.

The name Peter Toole was written on the label of the folder. He opened it, and began reading. It was the transcript of the interviews that had taken place five years previously, when he was charged.

He felt a twinge of curiosity. There had been something a bit odd about this case. Why had those low-lifes been so adamant about the younger brother's involvement? Glancing across at the newspaper, he noticed in surprise a photo of that same person. Checking the file, he confirmed that it was Ben. His eyes glanced towards another heading on the same page. He scratched his head and a strange sensation went up his spine.

Detective O'Reilly was now middle aged and balding, but had been quite good looking in his youth and quite the ladies' man. It was his single mindedness, a certain relentlessness; combined with his insightful knowledge of human frailty that helped him to solve cases so successfully. He thought back to the Peter Toole case, and it crossed his mind that the solution had been a little too easy.

He began to flick through the pages and read the transcripts of the interviews. Then, in a flash, it dawned on him that it would have been impossible for Tooley to have been in the car with Jimmy when the accident had happened. Pirate J had said he might have seen him around the time of the accident in the bus shelter, but that the person he saw was wearing a hoodie and he couldn't be absolutely certain it was him. He had talked about Tooley to a local teacher too, who didn't have a good word to say about him, an oddbod called Bates. Apparently, he was now in a psychiatric wing suffering from delusional psychosis. Strange, he might have been odd, but not that odd.

'Something strange about all this?' he pondered to himself. Then the telephone rang.

'There's been a report about a robbery at the pottery factory.'

'Oh shit, more work,' he thought.

He grabbed his coat and made his way to his car, which was parked outside the police station. He drove out of the town towards Port Lar. As he passed the railway station he started, recognising a familiar face in the young man walking along. It was Ben, trudging with a rucksack on his back, looking pale and tired.

'Hey, it's Ben isn't it? I'll give you a lift if you like,' he shouted as he wound the window down.

Ben looked towards him and replied, 'Thanks, yeah that would be great.'

As they drove along O'Reilly began to make small talk. 'What are you doing with yourself?'

At first Ben made no reply, then after a long pause mumbled, 'Uni, research, here's my house, thanks for the lift.'

Without ado he got out the car and headed down the lane.

'A bit odd,' thought Detective O'Reilly.

Ben thought the old house seemed less welcoming, perhaps because he had forgotten how the wind howled around the roof. He threw his bags into the hall and made his way to the kitchen.

He found a bottle of Peroni in the fridge and drank it. Tired from his journey, he guzzled a hastily made sandwich. He could hear his mother running down the stairs.

'Ben, I can't believe it's you, I've missed you so much!' She tried to give him a hug but her arm was in a sling from a recent fall.

'What happened to you, Mum, are you okay?'

'Am fine I just tripped over that chest of your dad's and managed to cut my arm on the edge. Hey, I am so sorry to hear about your friend Ahmed.' then she said, 'You look terrible! It must have been such a shock.'

'Oh that chest yes, mmm, is it still in dad's study?' he replied. Grace was taken aback at his brusqueness, and assumed he was trying to change the subject.

'Oh! No, I put it in the garage.'

Before she finished her sentence he had scurried off.

The chest had been placed in the corner of the garage

and was covered by an old blanket. As he fumbled for the light, a few little scurries of tiny feet could be heard as the mice nestled in the folds retreated to safety.

The chest, although very much worse for wear, was still in one piece and the contents were intact. Ben breathed a sigh of relief. He rummaged through it and found an old notebook, marked 'Theoretical Displacement'. He stuffed it into his pocket and returned to the house. Feeling tired he retreated to his old bedroom. Feeling rather disorientated, he lay on his bed, closed his eyes and fell asleep.

The next day, he began to read his father's notes in the belief that they would lead to some way forward. There had to be explanations and reasons. Given recent occurrences, he felt he was losing control of his mind and was beginning to panic. Acting on some kind of compulsion he could not explain, he decided to retrace his steps to the rocky cliffs where he had had the strange experience, all those years ago.

His presence in the village hadn't gone unnoticed. The station master was a friend of Tooley. That night in the local pub he had met up with him. 'Hey Tooley, Ben Ericson is back, saw him get off the train this afternoon.'

Tooley said nothing, fixing his glare of hate to the floor.

'Yeah, back home from that fancy university.'

He'd been working at the garage for some time now. Although he had been in trouble for his seedy dealings, he had tried to better himself. Working at the garage had its compensations. It had given him plenty of opportunities to get to know Amy, although he realised that his chances with her were slim.

When he had first started working at the garage, Amy

simply played with him, aware that her charms could work on most men and this boy was easy prey.

He had become quite infatuated for months, dreaming about her constantly. One day when they were alone at the garage he moved in close and grabbed hold of her arm. Amy had been aware of his gaze, idly delighting in the power she had over him, but there had been no physical contact until this point. Amy was taken aback.

'What are you doing?' she snapped.

Instantly he let go of her arm, asking awkwardly, 'Fancy going down to the tavern with me on Saturday, There's a band on should be good.' She wasn't really interested in him but didn't want to hurt his feelings.

She replied, 'I'll have to ask my dad, but yes, ok.'

'Right, I'll pick you up at eight!'

She was far from committed to this date. Amy was still fond of Ben and had been looking forward to the possibility of running into him during his holidays. She decided that if the date with Tooley did not go well she could always wander off and leave him at any time and be with her other friends. Everyone was celebrating the fact that the exams were finished and it was time to have some fun.

Tooley picked her up promptly at eight. He arrived in his car, which looked immaculate. He looked smart and well scrubbed, although there was still an odour of grease about him. Amy was casually dressed in her tight jeans and skimpy top. She had long blonde hair which seemed to fall perfectly around her shoulders. She had wide blue eyes and a perfectly formed face, lit by her wide attractive smile.

Down at the pub, Tooley wasted no time parading his catch in front of his mates. At first this seemed quite innocent but as the evening wore on she began to tire of his advances. With a shock she noticed Ben sitting by himself in a corner. He looked pale and depressed. The other kids seemed to ignore him. Bumping into Robbie, she asked, 'Ben doesn't look well, do you know what's wrong?'

'I dunno, he's changed, he's no fun anymore. Maybe you could talk to him or something,' he replied and wandered off, shaking his head. Making the excuse of going to get some crisps from the bar she headed straight for him. Perching on the seat next to him she tried to get him talking. He didn't seem to give much in reply so she put her arm around him flirtatiously. This did not go unnoticed by Tooley. He lumbered over to the couple, trying to look unconcerned, so as not to lose face.

'Amy, are you coming with us? We're going on to the Wellington,' he barked.

'I think I'd rather stay here, thanks,' she replied

At that moment Tooley grabbed Ben momentarily. 'Weirdo!' he hissed.

Sensing that things could get out of hand. Amy jumped up and said, 'Leave him alone! Ok, I'm coming,' and she agreed to go with him. 'Bye Ben, maybe see you later.'

He gave her a listless half smile.

She went to the Wellington, where the alcohol flowed, in addition to various other substances. The Wellington was a seedy old pub, which had become notorious for fights and drugs. Inside, Tooley was becoming increasingly obnoxious. Alcohol didn't do him any favours. Returning from a game of darts, she found him slumped in a corner

'I'm going home,' she said, angry with herself for having agreed to all this.

'Aw, you're no fun. I'll give you a lift though,' he slurred, his eyes dulled with drink.

'No way! I'll get a taxi,' she replied. Tooley tried to follow her but was overcome by a vomiting fit, which left him doubled over in the a corner of the car park

'You're so disgusting!' she shouted back as she left.

When she got home her dad was waiting for her.

'Had a good night? How come Tooley didn't bring you back?'

'He's an idiot, and no it wasn't much fun.'

Her dad was relieved, as he hoped for better things for her than a life with Tooley. 'Put it down to experience, love, that kid has always been a bit of a loser!'

She felt annoyed at being compromised by Tooley, and wished she had tried a little harder to console Ben.

# AMY

That year the summer months went by in a flash. As Autumn approached, most of the young people in the village were getting ready to go back to college or university. Many would venture far and wide from the island. Amy had set her sights on a career in nursing some time ago, pleased to be able to complete most of the training in Christchurch General Infirmary, which was conveniently not too far from Port Lar.

'Well love, you will be able to come home most weekends, or I could drive over and we could have dinner sometimes, what d'ya think?' Her dad was pleased she wouldn't be too far away.

'That would be great, Dad.' She knew he would be quite alone without her.

The training course had been quite intensive, and every hour of the day seemed filled. Despite this, she felt she had found her vocation. After qualifying she had settled into a flat with another nurse called Mary, who was from Ireland. She was slightly built and quite short. Her straight hair hung limply around her face. She had penetrating deep blue eyes which seemed to twinkle whenever she had a juicy tale to tell. Her wry wit and raucous laugh were very endearing, although her strong Cork accent was sometimes a little hard to decipher.

One night, just as she had got in from a long shift, Mary came running up to her.

'What's wrong, slow down, Mary. What's happened?'

'Dere's bin a phone call Amy, an emergency. It's yer daddy, he's had an accident!'

'What! Oh my God, where, what?'

'Now don't worry, he's in A&E!'

She grabbed her coat and went back to the hospital. She collared the receptionist, who she knew quite well, 'Could you tell me where Mike Rosser is? He's my dad!'

'Oh, they have taken him to x-ray. Seems he broke his leg, I heard them say he was a mechanic or something. Hope he's okay, Amy.'

'Thanks for your help,' She rushed along the corridor and found him in a wheelchair, looking a little sorry for himself.

'Dad! If you wanted to see me you didn't have to go and break your leg.' She smiled.

'Oh, Amy love, so glad to see you,' he gave her a hug.

He seemed more fragile than usual. She sighed to herself, realising she would have to make the journey back to Port Lar more often. It wouldn't be easy to fit this into her busy schedule at the hospital, but there wasn't really an alternative.

That evening she had a long heart to heart with Mary about the situation. Mary could see that she was compromised and tried to help saying, 'You know, Amy, you're going to be exhausted coming and going'

'Yes, I am, but he just doesn't seem to cope, I don't know what to do.'

'Oh, you poor soul,' Mary tried her best to comfort her and offered to swap shifts whenever she could. Amy had dutifully gone back and forth from Christchurch to Port Lar. However, it had become an onerous task and she knew it couldn't last.

Fortunately, a few weeks later a solution had presented itself. Mary spotted an advert in the newspaper for a nurse practitioner in Port Lar. She circled the advert and handed the newspaper to Amy.

'Look at this, perfect opportunity for you, go on, apply for it.'

Amy applied for the position. It would definitely solve a few problems for her. To her delight she was successful and within a couple of weeks found herself saying, 'I'm going to miss you, Mary.'

'Just make sure you come back soon.' Mary just smiled in a Mary sort of way.

Amy had told herself that this job would just be temporary, but somehow she felt she was being drawn back to the village.

Just before Christmas, as Amy was driving along the top road finishing her usual rounds, she saw a familiar figure walking along in the distance. It could only be one person and that was Ben. Drawing level, she called out to him in fun. 'Oh Ben, Ben, Ben. Ben Ericson is that you?'

Ben looked up and for a moment his face lit up, he was more than happy to see her but could not find a reply. He just continued on his way, turning down the lane to the shore. Amy was saddened by his lack of interest but also concerned. She thought she would check on him later. She would be going down to the big house to tend to his mother who had fallen and needed new dressings for a nasty wound.

Ben carried on down towards the sea. His mind was in a whirl. He looked at the distant horizon and had a strong sense that something was calling him.

The path along the cliffs was now quite overgrown. He pushed his way through the prickly briars and nettles. He found the spot where he had sat all those years ago and pulled out his dad's notebook from his pocket.

The notebook was leather bound and had a pencil down its spine. He held the pencil and began to flick through the pages. He saw a heading on one page which was underlined several times, 'Quantum Entanglement'. There were lots of scribbles and annotations. He turned to the next page, there were strange symbols and numerical equations. As he studied, there seemed to be the faintest of voices, calling to him on the wind. He looked up, but there was nothing.

Amy remembered that her last call was to the Ericson's house.

She drove into the drive and found Grace on the front step with her coat on.

'Where are you going, Mrs Ericson? You should be taking it easy for a while. That was a nasty injury.'

'Oh, Amy, you haven't by any chance seen Ben have you?'

'Well as a matter of fact I saw him this morning heading for the shore.'

'Well he should have been back ages ago. I'm just worried sick about him.'

'Why don't we go inside and have a cup of tea and we

can have a chat about it? I could sort out your dressing at the same time.'

'Ok, yes, that would be a good idea.' Amy made Grace some tea and took her into the lounge where they sat and talked.

'I think he's taken it really hard about his friend from uni, you know, Ahmed.'

'What happened to Ahmed?'

'Apparently, he is still in the hospital. He had an accident in the lab, tripped and banged his head. Ben was the last person to have talked to him.'

Amy thought to herself that might account for his demeanour earlier on. 'Don't worry, I'll go back by the shore on my way back and see if I can find him. Do you want me to tell your uncle?'

'Yes, thanks Amy, you are a sweetheart.' She hugged Amy and went to lie down on the couch.

Amy drove back down to the shore but could not see any sign of Ben. She called into the pub where she found Uncle George chatting away to some stranger.

'Hello there, Amy, what can I do for the prettiest nurse in the district?' He turned and winked at her. She smiled and said, 'You old charmer, be good now!' She sat down on the bar stool. She was tired and it had been a long day.

'Have you seen Ben? Gracie seems really anxious about him.'

A stranger then butted in. 'Do you mean Ben Ericson?'

'Yes, do you know him?' she replied

'Yes I do, and it's Detective O'Reilly, pleased to meet you.'

She looked startled and then it dawned on her that he was probably investigating the incident at the pottery, 'Oh, well I'm just trying to find him. His mother is very anxious about him.'

'As a matter of fact, I gave him a lift home earlier. Where has he gone then?'

'Down to the shore. He's feeling quite upset I think,' she replied. 'Do you want to tell me a little bit more about it? I do know the family.' George I'll have half a lager, and give the young lady whatever she wants.' They sat in the cubby hole and Amy told him all about Ben.

# PLANET NEON/ THE CLANDESTINE MEETING

Mi had returned home to gather her thoughts and refresh. She felt anxious and for the first time in her life resentful of the Directive. She stared into the reflection and noticed with a start that someone was behind her.

'What, what are you doing? Who are you? CORA initiate security!' She cried in alarm.

'I've temporarily disabled the domestic function. I need to speak with you urgently,' the figure replied.

She turned around, and was unable at first to see the intruder because she was hidden.

'Who are you, what do you want?' Mi asked in alarm. The figure began to emerge from beneath an invisibility shield. Mi was taken aback to see a young Calfarian girl.

'What are you doing here? Calfarians are not allowed in this zone!' she snapped abruptly.

'My name is Marli, Quilliam and I, well it's a long story,' she began, unsure how Mi would react, but there was no time for Seronian etiquette.

'What do you know about Quilliam?' Mia interjected.

'I know he is in great danger and that we must do something.'

Mi began to tremble, experiencing fears that were alien to her.

'But you are from the Forbidden Zone. How did you get in here and what do you mean danger, and how could you know Quilliam?' Mia gushed, but then remembered. 'You are the Calfarian from the Star Dome! You have some explaining to do!'

'I'm able to TP Quilliam. He doesn't understand where he is or what he has to do. He keeps finding himself in a place that is a long way from here, and he is trying to find his way back to us.'

Mi was so anxious she suddenly forgot all the protocols. She sat down and began to gather her thoughts.

'How has all this come about? How can you know these things?'

'I don't know. Quilliam told me he had been re-evaluated and it felt like he was very scared.'

Mi could sense that Marli was genuine, instinctively knowing that she would have to take her at her word.

'Give me a moment, I need to contact Pedan.'

'Be careful, the Directive will be watching your every move.'

'I'll encrypt it, he will be the only one who could decipher it.'

'I must go now. Will you wait here?'

'No! I'm coming too!' replied Mi.

They slipped out unnoticed under the guise of the invisibility shield.

In the empty apartment, Cora reanimated and could be heard saying, 'Malfunction anomaly, system reboot.'

# ORB 1

At the orb there had been a great deal of activity. VERA was hovering around Quilliam's capsule checking the life support system. 'VERA, explain the anomaly,' Pedan commanded.

'There's been a spike in the entanglement,' it replied. 'There are indications that the subject Quilliam experienced an irregularity. The sensors are detecting synaptic overload.'

'How can this be? Why Quilliam?' Pedan looked deeply concerned.

'We are increasing sedation in order to maintain function.'

Pedan retired back to his workstation, shocked and horrified. He suspected there was more to this. If he was to help Quilliam, he had to have his wits about him and think logically. He dreaded having to explain the situation to Mi. Then he looked into his communicator. He could see that there was an amber communication. It was then that he saw the encrypted ciphertext.

It was from Mi, reading, 'Meet me at Alpha Station 1 ... urgent.' He wondered why she was behaving in such a clandestine manner. He had to find her and tell her what the situation was.

It would be difficult to leave the area unnoticed but there was little time to lose.

'VERA, maintain observation.' He commanded 'I will return in forty-five, I need recess.' This seemed acceptable to VERA, who turned towards Quilliam and began to make further diagnostic assessments. Pedan then proceeded to the vestibule and made his exit.

VERA responded, 'Authorising a window of forty-five for reinvigoration. Science Officer Pedan.'

Mi and Marli had made their way to Alpha Station 1. They mingled with the personnel and waited for Pedan to arrive. There was a lot of unusual activity in the area. On a large screen above the transport area the Mahon was making an announcement.

'Citizens of Neon, please do not be alarmed, but for your safety we request that you return to your zones. There is a disturbance in the bio stratosphere and we will be initiating a freeze down.'

'Oh no, it's a zone shutdown! What can we do?' Marli asked, feeling anxious.

'Don't worry, Marli, I've thought of something,' said Mi.

At that moment Pedan arrived. 'Mi, who is this?' He looked inquisitively at Marli.

'I'll explain later, can you imprint a Zone 1 onto Marli's identifier?' There was a sense of purpose and authority about Mi that he had not seen before.

'I can try, what identity can she assume?'

'I've already thought about that, she can be Senna 985, do you remember I made two tags when we collected Quilliam from the natal chamber? One male, one female.'

'Ok, good thinking, but we must act quickly, I must return

before my revig time ends. I can make the adjustment at the portal, but it might be a permanent transfer. You might not be able to return to your own family and zone afterwards.'

'I can't think about that now, just do it!' said Marli.

# PLANET EARTH/PORT LAR

Ben staggered home through the front door looking very unwell. Grace managed to get him onto the sofa. His eyes were bloodshot and his face twitching. At that moment, Amy knocked on the door. 'Just let yourself in, we are in the lounge,' called Grace breathlessly.

Amy came in, knelt down by the sofa and studied the expression on Ben's face. He was barely aware of her, muttering something under his breath.

'What's he saying?' said Grace.

'Not sure, sounded like "Dad"?'

The blood seemed to drain from Grace's face and she looked deathly pale.

'Oh my God! That's what this is all about!' said Amy.

'I, I don't know' Grace suspected a repeat of the same old mystery.

'I think he's somehow trying to find his dad. Do you think he could be suffering from some sort of delayed grief?' said Amy.

Grace nodded sadly in silence.

They heard the sound of a car rolling along the gravel driveway and Grace looked through the window. She called out to Amy.

'There's someone at the door. I'll get it, you stay with Ben.'

'I think it's Detective O'Reilly. Why would he come here now?'

Grace rushed to the front door and let him in, 'Detective O'Reilly! I haven't seen you for a while'

'Just thought I'd have a chat, Mrs Ericson. Is Amy here too?'

'Yes, she's in the lounge with Ben.'

She escorted him into the lounge. Amy was sitting with Ben, who was now beginning to look a little better.

'How's he doing?' he asked Amy while looking closely at Ben.

'Well, his pulse seems to be back to normal. I think he needs to get a thorough check up. I'll make an appointment with the doctor and we can see what this is all about.'

'Good idea, maybe tomorrow when he's feeling more himself we could have a chat?'

'I'm sure that would be fine, would you both like some tea?'

'No, better go, got to catch up on my paperwork.'

'Me too, I need to go back to the clinic.'

Grace showed them both to the front door and thanked them for their concern. She managed to get Ben to his feet and walked him to his bedroom. He flopped onto his bed. She removed his shoes and socks and lifted his legs into a horizontal position and pulled the covers over him. As he lay his head back onto the pillow she kissed his forehead and said, 'Get some rest, my darling boy, we'll get to the bottom of all this.'

Her heart was heavy with a sense of foreboding. Ben drifted off into a fitful sleep, filled with strange dreams.

When he awoke he found himself holding onto the rudder of their little cruiser, heading for the Emerald Rocks. He had no idea how he had come to be there.

# EARTH SCIENCE SURVEILLANCE

The following day Detective O'Reilly went back to his office in Christchurch. There was an envelope on the table marked URGENT. He sighed, thinking that this must be another of those official warnings. He was often at loggerheads with his superiors.

He grabbed a coffee and sat back in his chair. After he had gathered his thoughts, he opened the envelope. Inside was a file marked CONFIDENTIAL. He gasped when he saw the name Ben Ericson and his photograph on the first page. The document had been sent to him from ESS Service (Earth Science Surveillance).

Then his mobile phone began to ring. He frantically searched for it, eventually finding it at the bottom of his briefcase.

'Hello, is that Detective O'Reilly?'

'Yes that's me, who am I talking to?' said O'Reilly

'My name is Jonathan Holt, I work with ESS, have you received the file I sent you?'

'Yes, I've only just opened it. What is all this fuss about Ben Ericson?' He felt a little out of his depth.

'It's a long story, we have had Ben Ericson and his father under our radar for some years, in connection with events which are classified. I need to meet with you urgently.

Could you please arrange some accommodation for me and, most importantly, can you keep this information to yourself?'

'Yes, of course, when do you need to be here?'

'Tomorrow will be fine, I'll be on the first train, meet me at the station, I'll ring again.' The phone clicked off.

'Oh Jesus, what is this all about?' wondered O'Reilly in utter confusion. He stowed the file and then instructed his secretary to make accommodation plans for his guest.

'Is it someone from the head office?' said Fran. Fran had worked at the station for over thirty years and she liked to think that she was in charge, although her efficiency was not what it was.

'Afraid so!' was his improvised reply.

'Oh! no, my filing! Oh drats, the only week when I haven't sorted it all out, we get this thrown at us! Typical of them upstairs!' She began to mutter and tidy up sheaves of paper.

'Don't worry about it, he's going to be going on an investigation with me,' He tried in vain to calm her down.

'Don't worry! Don't worry!' she cried. 'I want to make sure I get my pension! I've been tidying up after you, you scruffy B, for years.' She ranted in similar fashion for quite some time, but O'Reilly left her to it, knowing that she would have everything pristine in the end. 'Hmm, yes the pottery thing. Gotta go I'll call in later,' he called, as he proceeded to make a quick exit to avoid any further lambasting.

'Typical of him he just goes off on one of his flights of fancy leaving me to sort everything out.'

O'Reilly bundled the files into his briefcase and headed for his car.

'Something very odd going on,' he thought to himself.

He decided to head for Port Lar. He took the coast road. It was a clear day, he glanced out through the window of the car and looked across at the bay. He saw a little motor cruiser speeding across it. He decided to park the car on the headland where he could get a good view. He took his binoculars out of the glove compartment and watched the little boat. Suddenly he started in recognition.

'What the F..k!' he muttered.

He made out that it was Ben at the wheel of the boat. It was heading in the direction of the Emerald Rocks. He thought to himself, 'What now? What's the fascination with those rocks? Is he hiding something there?'

He returned to his car and headed for the village. As he passed by the store he saw that Amy was parked there. She came out of the shop with a plastic bag full of groceries.

'Excuse me, Amy, can I have a word?' he called over, startling her.

'Why are you here? I thought you were going back to Christchurch,' she said in surprise.

'I think we need to have a little talk.' He smiled, trying to put her at ease.

'Ok, as long as you promise not to arrest me. My dad wants his tea!' she joked.

'No, don't be daft, maybe I could come to your house. Would your dad mind?' He knew he was being a little bit forward with his request.

'No problem! My dad will love the company. We live just by the garage in North Street. I'll see you there in five minutes.'

'Great, thanks.' Pleased that she was so obliging, he

began to feel that this was not going to be the kind of investigation he was used to.

When he arrived at the garage he found Amy's dad tinkering with an old Triumph motorcycle.

'Wow, haven't seen one of those for years.' He was intrigued.

'Yep, she's a beauty alright, 1968 model. Er ... can I help you?'

'Oh, sorry, my name is Detective O'Reilly. Amy invited me.'

'Oh right, yes, well just let me get this sorted and I will be with you.' He was curious as to why Amy had invited him over.

'So, you're trying to sort out the pottery break in, bloody idiots.'

'Well yes, but I'm also trying to find out a little bit more about young Ben Ericson.'

Amy's dad looked surprised. 'Ben's a good kid, bit of a loner, doubt he would be your suspect,' he laughed

At that moment Amy arrived.

'Oh I see you have met my dad. Come on into the house, otherwise he will have you polishing that old heap of rubbish!'

He followed her into the house, which was cluttered with all kinds of memorabilia.

'I see your dad must have done a lot of racing in his time.' He picked up a silver trophy from the mantelpiece.

'Yes, I guess it's his passion. Anyway, how can I help you?'

'I need some information about Ben Ericson. I believe you and he know each other?'

He fixed his gaze on her, making her feel slightly uncomfortable.

'Yes, we were at school together. I've always liked him. Although he seems to have changed recently.'

'In what way?' he interrupted her.

'Well, I don't know how to explain it, but somehow he just doesn't seem to be himself at all. It was such a shock for him when his brother died, you know, in that freak accident, and then he never really knew his dad, only Frank.'

'What happened to his father?'

'Oh, he was the guy that disappeared. Grace never got over it, they were really close. Anyway, would you like some tea?'

'Yes, that would be great. By the way, I think I might have just seen Ben in a boat going across the bay, is that usual?'

'Well, it's not so unusual. He often used to go fishing off the rocks. In fact, if I remember rightly, there was a strange incident there once. Come to think of it, I suppose that's when it all seemed to go a bit pear shaped.'

As she couldn't really offer any other explanations, O'Reilly felt that was his cue to leave.

'Thanks for the tea. I think I might just go down to the shore and have a look around. Maybe catch up with you again sometime!'

'No problem, glad to be of help. I'll be visiting his mom again tomorrow so I should be able to find out how he is.' She escorted him to the front door, after which he got into his car and headed to the beach.

# THE ROCK

Ben stared feverishly into the distance as he navigated the cruiser towards the Emerald Rocks. His heart seemed to pound in his chest and he felt quite breathless. There was a strange silence to the air, which was unusually calm. The boat bobbed up and down as it crossed the swirling currents flowing in around the rocks.

The waves lapped against the shore. A flurry of opportunistic seabirds encircled the cruiser and then drifted back onto the high ledges of approaching cliffs. Grey clouds were clustering together, leaving only a patch of blue visible. He had been to this place many times so it was familiar to him, although he still had no memory of how he came to be here on this day. He steered around the north side and made fast to the landing stage, feeling a little light-headed.

He alighted from the boat and walked to the shore, making his way to a large boulder by a sandy cove. The boulder had always been referred to as the 'Giant's Rock', as it seemed to stand incongruously in the sand, quite out of place compared to the rest of the rocks that surrounded it. There were many stories about it.

The most outlandish story being that it was rolled there by a giant millions of years ago. This had given rise to its name although, almost as strangely, it was actually a fragment of a meteor which had landed there thousands of years previously. He sat down by the boulder and let his mind drift.

Gradually, everything around him seemed to take on a different hue. He felt a strange energy emanating from the rock behind him. Turning, he placed his hands on the soft shiny surface, which felt to him as though it was softly vibrating. He glanced out towards the sea, noticing that a thick mist was coming inland. It began to snake towards him from across the bay. He noticed that something seemed to be disturbing the water. There were strange ripples which were moving rapidly towards him. He felt as if they were hypnotising him. There seemed to be a strange pressure against his chest. The air was heavy, as if charged with electricity. He could hardly breathe and held his hands to his chest as his respiration became more and more laboured.

At that moment, a watery blue shape rose from the water in front of him. Its translucent form snaked its way out of the sea and along the shore. Particles of sand seemed to be attracted to it and covered its surface. A humanoid shape began to reveal itself. Slightly larger than him in size, it now stood directly in front of him staring directly into his eyes. Even though it did not move, it seemed to push him backwards against the rock. Then his weightless body seemed to fall, not against the rock but into it. The sandy shape dissipated away in front of his eyes. Now he was inside the boulder, looking out to a space in front which seemed to open before him. He found himself walking down a long tunnel, following someone or something.

He could hear a ringing sound in his ears and a strange dazzling sensation in his eyes, although there was no bright light to be seen. He found himself in some kind of chamber that was enclosed with iridescent walls.

He tried desperately to say something, but he did not seem to be able to make any sound. He wasn't sure whether or not he was saying the words himself but words seemed to appear, echoing and distant. Strange images seemed to flash through his mind. He sensed something hovering close to him, beckoning him closer. Although he could not see it, it felt as though two arms were being wrapped around him. It triggered a memory of being cradled. He felt no fear. On the contrary, he felt protected and deeply calm. Gradually he became aware of a human shape embracing him. He recognised the features to be those of his father. 'Dad?' he asked.

Then there was a roar in his ears and all seemed to go black.

He woke up face down, lying in front of the boulder. Dazed by his experience, he also took strength from it. All the strange events he had experienced that were beyond his control now began to feel benign rather than sinister. He turned his hands upwards and saw that there were some strange bloodied impressions on his fingertips. He assumed he must have used his hands to break his fall against the boulder. He noticed that there were some strange indentations in the sand leading up to the water's edge. Feeling overwhelmed, he had a strong desire to experience simple normal things, things that he could understand, and resolved to leave as quickly as he possibly could. He clambered into the boat, and with what strength he had left, managed to get the outboard motor going. Then he pointed the little cruiser in the direction of the harbour and sped across the bay. As he approached the landing stage, he could see there was a figure waiting for him. It was O'Reilly.

'Ah, Ben, just the person I wanted to talk to! What happened to you? Did you have a fall or something? You've got a lot of bruising around your eyes.'

He tried to explain but his words made no sense.

'I'll take you home, Ben. You don't seem yourself and your mother will be worried.'

He bundled him into his car and took him back to the house.

Grace was alerted to their arrival by the sound of the car in the driveway. She rushed to the door. O'Reilly had his arm around Ben, almost having to carry him toward the house.

'Oh my God, what has happened? Has he had an accident?' asked Grace anxiously.

'I think he must have fallen or something. I am sure he will be okay, but better just put him to bed and let him recover. Maybe get Amy to look at him in the morning.'

They both manhandled him up the stairs and into his bedroom.

Ben lay on his bed and murmured, 'I'll be fine, just let me alone for a bit.'

With that they simply left him to it.

He put the plug in the sink and turned on the tap. The warm water seemed to soothe his fingertips. He then looked up into the mirror. He could hardly recognise himself, his eyes were swollen. Then as he looked closely he could see that their appearance had somehow changed.

'Shit, what's happening to me?' he muttered.

He then turned over his fingers and touched the cold porcelain sink. He felt it vibrating beneath his fingertips. Shaken, he made his way back to his bed quickly and fell into an exhausted sleep.

Grace peered into Ben's room to check on him. Noticing how deeply asleep he was, she left him alone and simply gazed down at him.

'Oh Yan, what is happening to our boy?' She sighed and wiped a tear away from her eye.

Detective O'Reilly was waiting for her in the front room.

'Ah, there you are, has he settled down now?'

'I hope so,' she replied. Feeling a need to explain his actions, she said, 'You see, it's been so hard for him, what with losing his father and his brother, and it not working out between Frank and me.'

O'Reilly interrupted her, 'Don't upset yourself, we'll get to the bottom of it somehow.'

'Maybe you should get some rest yourself. Perhaps call round tomorrow to see how things are.'

'Thanks, that's very considerate of you.'

She led him to the door and watched him get into his car. As he drove, he thought he'd just call in at the local pub on his way back. He glanced down at his phone and could see that there had been several messages left for him

Firstly it was his secretary – 'Urgent, get back to the office. ESS have called three times!'

Secondly it was the ESS. A meeting had been arranged for 10 pm tomorrow.

'Damn!' he thought. He put his foot on the accelerator

and sped off down the road. He needed to catch up with his paperwork, especially now that this crowd were coming to town. As he drove around the harbour he noticed several boats forming what seemed to be a circle in the harbour. Their searchlights seemed to be fixed on one point and in the air a helicopter was hovering.

'What the hell is going on now?' he thought.

# PLANET – NEON

Mi looked anxiously at Pedan and said, 'Has something happened in the orb?'

'I hesitate to say this but things are definitely not going well.' Pedan could not hide his unease. 'If we are to get Quilliam out of there, then time is of the essence!'

Mi felt alarmed. 'Pedan you have to trust me and tell me what has happened! We must move quickly. We will be monitored if we are not careful.'

'Yes, of course, if we take the next shuttle we can get off at Section B,' said Marli.

'I know an aqua-tunnel that connects with the main sphere.'

'How do you know that, I thought you couldn't enter any A Zones!'

Marli laughed. 'We don't all do as we are told. Where there is a will, there is a way. By the way are you able to swim?'

'It's been a long time, I last did so when I took my sub-aqua merits.' She fiddled with her earclips, not wanting to show her disdain at being challenged by a Calfarian.

'You will have to remove those,' remarked Marli, smiling

Mi grimaced, but this wasn't the time to argue so she did as she was bid.

Pedan's brow furrowed as he contemplated the next course of action.

'Ok, the shuttle is approaching, let's go!' With that they were on board and being transported to Section B. They huddled together, Marli covered by her invisibility shield, to avoid recognition. At one intersection an imaging device seemed to be scanning them. Marli was convinced that the alarm would be activated, but it stayed silent.

Finally, they reached the stop. As the occupants headed for the exit the three of them hung back until the last was through, then they ran as fast as they could in the opposite direction. This led them to the maintenance level, where the aqua tunnel was located. Marli used her retina pattern to activate the door.

'How did you do that?' Pedan looked at her inquisitively.

'Oh, done it loads of time, are you ready? JUMP!'

Mi closed her eyes and took a deep breath and jumped, followed by Pedan. They found themselves in the swirling waters of the aqua. They felt a burning sensation as their lungs adjusted to the pressure and force of the water. Marli swam confidently above them like a dolphin guiding its babies and navigated them to a ledge beneath a shaft which led up to the orb.

They hurled themselves up onto the ledge. Mi looked up at the shaft, which seemed to go on forever.

'Do we have to climb?' Marli looked hesitant.

'Am afraid so, there is no time to lose. The sensors will soon detect our presence. Don't worry I'm right behind you.'

Mi took a few hesitant steps but then gradually became more confident. It was an exhausting climb. She concentrated on looking upwards and with every breath took another step, her heart pounding. They were all finding breathing difficult and laboured upwards in agony. The climb seemed to go on forever. At last, to their relief, a shining, spherical shape was beginning to appear in the distance. They were now within reach of a service hatch that opened into the internal corridors of the sphere.

Marli pushed upwards for one final time, then shouted, 'Quick, quick open the hatch Pedan!' Pedan reached out, and pushed the hatch with all his might. There was a 'whooshing' sound and then it slowly opened. At that moment he glanced down and he could see the menacing glow of a fleet of aqua drones, scrambling up towards them along the wall of the shaft.

Pedan felt sick with fear as he imagined what their fate could have been. Landing in a heap in the corridor, Pedan closed the hatch just in time. If the aqua drones had caught up with them they would have dragged them back into the swirling waters, where they would have been drowned and minced to pieces.

They picked themselves up and started to walk. They were now in one of the lower access corridors. These led up to the engineering shafts and ultimately to the orb and sphere. Marli spoke first. 'Well we have got this far, we can do it.' She gave Mi a comforting hug. Pedan looked ahead anxiously. There was a humming sound up ahead.

'I think I know where we are,' he said, becoming quite agitated.

'Listen!' In the background, a distinct rhythmic vibration seemed to reverberate through the corridor.

'That's the quantum probe!' muttered Pedan.

'What does that mean?' asked Marli looking concerned.

'It means the chamber is above us. Pedan, do you think they are active now?' Mi asked, looking anxious.

Pedan did look worried.

'Yes, but we can still retract the probe if I can get to the control,' he said, his voice quivering a little.

'Which way now?' asked Marli.

'Straight on, we will need to get past the security. Have you still got the cloaking device?' Pedan looked at Mi, who searched through the pockets of her tunic. She was relieved to find that the little square device was still attached to the lining.

'Ok, let's go!' In an instant they were invisible and began to make their way along the corridor to the next level. The corridors had various access doors. The markings on the doors indicated the direction. Pedan had an access implant which enabled them to move freely. Eventually they reached what Pedan assumed was the Diodem chamber. The doors to the chamber were askew. Tentatively, they slipped inside undetected.

Pedan led the way, heading for the control unit. They would need to employ some kind of diversionary tactic to enable him to reach it.

'Where is the emergency alarm located?' asked Marli.

'It's just over there by the work station. But you need the ...' before Pedan could finish his sentence Marli had abandoned the safety of the invisibility shield and was heading in the direction of the alarm.

Marli picked up a large metal flask and hurled it towards the alarm. Immediately all hell broke out in the chamber. Sirens sounded, lights flashed, and droids whizzed back and forth. As fast as she could, she ducked back under the shield, Mi grabbed her in relief.

'Don't do that again!'

Marli smiled at Mi, who feigned a scowl.

'Now let's get out of here. We have to get Quilliam!'

Pedan was now standing in front of the control. However, he wasn't alone. Several droids had surrounded him. He stood motionless.

A voice echoed around the chamber.

'Ah welcome Pedan, we have been waiting for you. It is time to make the final preparation.'

Pedan responded with, 'Yes of course.' There was a pause and then he said, 'I pledge my allegiance under oath to the Supreme Council.'

It seemed a strange thing for him to say at that moment.

Marli and Mi were heading down to the chamber where Quilliam was being held.

'We are not going to make it!' cried Mi.

'Yes we are. Run ... run!' Marli grabbed hold of Mi and they sped down the corridor to the chamber, which was brightly lit. There was a great deal of activity going on. Mi, trying as she might, couldn't keep up with Marli and slipped. As she lay on the ground now visible, she too was surrounded by droids. They lifted her up and placed her on a platform. She was then whisked away.

Fortunately, Marli was still hidden by the cloaking device. She was almost at the entrance, and could see Quilliam lying prostrate on a plinth, with various tubes connecting him to a machine.

Mi had been transported to a transparent cell within the chamber. She stood, looking on in horror at Quilliam's predicament. She then turned toward the control unit where Pedan was standing. He seemed to be about to initiate the quantum process. Mi banged on the windows of her cell, desperately trying to get Pedan's attention. He didn't seem to acknowledge her in any way. He was busy animating various procedures that seemed to cause Quilliam's body to quiver and twitch. The room was silent, with the High Council standing ominously on a platform above, watching his every move. Droids were standing motionless, guarding the exits.

'No. No! Pedan you can't do this to our son!' Mi screamed. The words echoed emptily around the chamber.

# PLANET EARTH

Back in Port Lar there were a large number of military vessels gathered in the bay. Helicopters were still circling, and the area of activity seemed to centre over the Emerald Rocks. These events had not gone unnoticed in the village.

The local fishermen had gathered in the Fisherman's Arms. Gathered around the bar, they were all grumbling about the fact that the fishing fleet had been temporarily grounded.

'Who do they think they are!'

'We're not going to stand for this! Once we let go of our rights to fish in those waters, we'll be finished! You'll see, come on lads we'll show 'em who is the boss!' shouted Frank, somewhat inebriated. He was often idly drunk, but now he had suddenly found himself with a purpose, in charge of an angry rabble. He was just about to lead them to take their demonstration onto the quay when Detective O'Reilly appeared.

He shouted over the noise, 'Look lads, it's inconvenient, but if you go against the military on this you are going to get yourselves into more trouble than you could possibly imagine. This is for your own safety. If there's something explosive in the water it's best to stay right away and let them get on with sorting it out. The alternative is that you can spend the night in a nice little cell down at the station. Do I make myself clear?'

There were a lot of grumbles and angry ripostes, but the general consensus was that they could not argue with a set of armed military vessels. 'Let's stay in the pub and start thinking about compensation claims,' Frank shouted, planning ahead. 'Aye,' there was an agreement on that.

Meanwhile, up at the house, Ben was trying to process what had happened to him. It seemed that he was increasingly unable to function as his normal self. Something beyond his own identity was driving him.

He lay on his bed staring up at the ceiling, experiencing confused emotions and thoughts. He glanced across his room to the bookcase and noticed a brown envelope tied with string.

'I wonder what that is?' he thought to himself.

He pushed his duvet back and sat on the edge of his bed, still feeling exhausted. He managed to summon up enough energy to walk across the room and grab the parcel. Going back to his bed he lay back against the soft pillow. It was a comforting place to be, everything from his childhood close around him. There was a box of old toys that his mother hadn't been able to throw out, his old school tie still hanging over the wardrobe door and his football boots stuffed under the bed.

He put the parcel on his lap and began to untie the string. It was addressed to him. On the back of the parcel he could clearly see the name of the sender.

Mr Bates, Flat 3, Peveril Street, Port Lar.

'This is very odd. Why would old Batesy be sending me a parcel?' thought Ben.

He pulled back the brown wrapping paper and found a worn and grubby black folder. A letter was attached with Sellotape to the outer cover. On the top edge of the file he noticed the initials Y E.

'That's my dad's initials! I wonder why Batesy had his folder?'

He began to read the letter.

*Dear Ben,*

*If you are reading this then I imagine something must have happened to me. I was going to post it to you a long time ago. I'm sorry to say that I have done a selfish thing. You see, all my life I dreamed of knowing about distant worlds. I came upon this folder quite by accident. I thought it was my destiny, how wrong could I be?*

*Well, I believe the information that lies within this folder was meant for you, my boy.*

*It was put together by your father. For what purpose I have no idea. I have pondered the contents and am delighted to send it to you now. Forgive me for holding on to it. I am just a curious old fool.*

*I wish you well, Ben, hope you find some answers here.*

*Yours sincerely,*

*Mr Bates*

Ben was flabbergasted. 'What, how could he?' Ben was angry, but also sad. He remembered that strange day in the lab. He was sorry that Mr Bates had had a stroke. It was the last day that he had seen him. Mr Bates had recovered, but appeared to have lost his reason. He had been sectioned, and was now in a psychiatric ward.

Ben had felt somehow responsible. He put the letter on

one side and held the folder. It felt strange to be holding something that had belonged to his dad. He felt almost tearful. He pulled himself together and began turning the pages. There were reams of scientific data, astronomical charts and historical articles about 'the Blue Men'. This caught his attention, particularly one drawing of a humanoid creature that seemed to inhabit a subterranean cave.

'That's what I saw! What's it got to do with my dad?'

He read on and found another section that was all about bioluminescent organisms. It mentioned a terrestrial mollusc, a Rosanthrocae. There was detailed analysis of its remarkable molecular structure. It discussed its habitat, and various diagrams seemed to indicate that it could be located in the subterranean caves below the Emerald Rocks.

Ben scratched his head, he was puzzled. It then dawned on him.

'I've seen one of those before as well! I'm sure it's in the study, in Dad's old sample box.'

He crept downstairs and went into the study. It was stuffed with books, boxes and some old bits of scientific equipment. He had often rummaged around in it when he was a child. On one of the top shelves there were some old leather bound boxes. They had the inscription 'YE Institute of Scientific Research'. He'd always been fascinated by them but hadn't been tall enough to reach them. He remembered that he had once tried to climb up the shelves to get to them, but his mother had caught him and had been very angry.

He remembered her saying, 'Those boxes are very special indeed. Your dad told me to look after them very carefully!'

He'd replied cheekily, 'What's inside?'

'It's a very rare sample that your dad was researching for the Institute. Now leave it where it is!' She was adamant that he should not touch it.

He looked around the study and saw that those same boxes were still on the shelf. He reached up and brought them down. The first box was full of test tubes and pipettes. He put that on one side. The second was quite different. There was a glass jar wrapped in muslin. It had a screw top lid on which was written 'Sample A, Rosanthropod.' Without knowing why, he unscrewed the jar, took out the shell, wrapped it in the muslin and put it in his pocket.

Filled with a sense of purpose he hardly understood, he then ran outside to the garage, looking for his old bike. He eventually found it hanging on a hook. He reached up, lifted it to the ground and sat on it. It was strange to be on it again after so long. He adjusted the seat until it felt comfortable for his height. Closing the door as quietly as he could, he wheeled the bike along the gravel drive, then he set off down the road. He could see in the distance that there was a lot of activity going on in the bay. There seemed to be a clear plan in his mind, although it did not seem to be of his making.

'Shit, shit! I'll never make it in time,' he muttered.

Suddenly, out of nowhere two bright headlamps seemed to be upon him. He tried to manoeuvre out of the way but skidded and fell forwards into the verge. Fortunately, the grass was long and the ground quite soft. He got up quite quickly with no injuries. He noticed that the vehicle had stopped and the driver was approaching him. A familiar figure approached, the very last person he needed to see at this moment. It was Tooley.

'Oh, bloody hell, sorry mate. Just didn't see you!,' said Tooley in a gruff voice.

'I'm alright, thanks.' Ben wanted to just get out of his way.

'It's Ben, isn't it?' Tooley stood staring at him. 'What are you doing?' He got even closer.

'I said I'm fine, can't stop, gotta go, get out of my way.' He tried to push past him

'Okay, okay calm down!' Tooley looked worried and then he stepped back. 'Don't you be doing that weird eyes thing on me!'

'I'm not doing anything weird. Look it's really important that I go.'

'You're in no fit state to go anywhere. Look mate, we have had our differences but that was a long time ago. That bike is fucked. Get in the car and I'll take you wherever you need to be.' Tooley seemed remarkably genuine.

'You're not going to like it,' replied Ben, standing by the car clinging onto his backpack.

'Try me!' said Tooley.

'Gotta get down to the other side of the rocks, without those guys seeing me.' He pointed to the boats in the bay, unsure as to why he had confided in Tooley.

'No problem,' said Tooley, smiling. It was suddenly like old times. He was thoroughly adept at sneaking around undetected. He wasn't going to be beaten by any authority.

'Isn't that Amy's dad's car?'

'It certainly is, the one and only Super Audi Quattro!!' He had managed to acquire it from Amy's dad and had made a few adjustments. It had four shining exhausts, a fancy spoiler on the back and bull bars on the front. As he put his foot down, the highly tuned engine roared, and they flew up the road.

'Got an idea!' Tooley cried.

'Look, you can't get involved. This could end up being dangerous,' said Ben, trying to extricate himself from him, but Tooley was determined, and now complicit. He also hadn't had as much excitement in years.

'You say you need to get to the other side of the rocks without being seen?'

'Yes.' Ben nodded grimly.

'No problem.' Tooley grinned from ear to ear, realising that he knew of a solution.

'There's an old mine shaft that leads directly to Devil's Cave.'

Ben looked at him in disbelief. Tooley nodded with a grin, then turned back to the controls of the car. He roared down the twisting lanes until they reached the side of the cliff.

'We gotta walk from here.'

'You don't have to come!' Ben said, trying to dissuade him yet again from following him.

'No chance, we're in this together!'

Ben was pleased that Tooley had taken him at his word and replied, 'Thanks, mate!'

They clambered up the side of the cliff. They pulled back the bracken and slithered along a thin slippery path until they reached a sign which read: 'Danger Open Mine Shaft. Strictly No Admittance'.

Tooley had been there several times before, as it was a good place to hide things. He pushed the wooden sign to one side and grabbed a rope which was attached to the inside wall of the shaft.

'It's a bit of a drop so watch yourself. Pass me that torch.'

Tooley shone the torch down the hole. Grabbing the rope, they descended down the steeply angled shaft into the darkness until they came to an overhang. They could see the remains of a ladder trailing down to the floor of the shaft.

'Ladder's bust, gonna have to climb down the last bit.'

They lowered themselves into the gloom, scabbling for holds as best they could. Ben touched the ground with relief, but Tooley slipped at the very end,

landing very heavily on his left ankle.

'Jesus Christ! Think I've done my fuckin' ankle in. Don't think I can walk. Sorry, Ben.'

'Look, just stay here and when I've got what I need I'll be back. Keep an eye out and don't let anyone follow me.' He gave Tooley a hug, which said everything that needed to be said. 'Be bloody careful, Ben,' he cried, watching him disappear into the darkness. 'You've got about an hour before the tide comes in,' he called, although Ben gave no sign of having heard him.

Ben followed the steep passage down to an opening which gradually opened out into a large cave looking out to sea. By the cave beach, he discovered an old rowing boat covered in a mossy old tarpaulin. He pulled the tarpaulin off and found a pair of oars underneath. He pushed the craft over along the rocks, to where there seemed to be a natural ramp down into the water. Shoving off into the water, his heart was pounding in his chest and he felt tired and faint. With what little energy he had left, he rowed as rapidly as he could towards the leeward side of the rocks. It was a blustery night and there seemed to be a lot of swell, forcing the dinghy to lurch violently from side to side.

Ahead, he could see a patch of water that seemed to be illuminated from beneath. It seemed to be forming some kind of vortex, drawing him inwards. The boat began to spin around rapidly. Helpless in the swirling waters, it gradually sank beneath the waves.

# PLANET NEON – THE DISCOVERY

Marli saw that Mi had been captured by the droids and taken into the orb. She darted away along the corridor and hid behind a column. There seemed to be a lot of activity going on in the main chamber. Trooper droids swept past but didn't seem to notice her. She edged her way along until she found a recess. Turning into it, she came across what seemed to be a pair of ornately carved doors. She had never seen anything like them before. They seemed incongruous in this clinical environment. She traced her hands over some of the elaborate carvings looking for some kind of opening mechanism. Looking upwards, she noticed an engraving at the top of the doors that read, 'May they rest for eternity'.

She pushed a catch hidden in the woodwork, and to her surprise the doors began to open slightly. She edged herself through and closed them behind her. The chamber she found herself in was dimly lit, but she could make out the outline of two plinths in the middle of the room. Each of the plinths supported a highly decorated capsule, shaped like a sarcophagus. She looked around the room and saw that it was highly decorated, with many adornments.

Forgetting her predicament for a moment, her curiosity got the better of her. She decided to climb one of the plinths and look more closely. Noticing that some steps lead upwards to its edge, she climbed them and stared in wonder at the ornate casket. She rested her hands upon the edge, then lay her head on top of it, listening intently.

Given that she was a natural telepath, she soon detected something trying to communicate, but the language was strange and unfamiliar. She was aware of its tone, however, which seemed both sincere and deeply beseeching.

The sarcophagus seemed to be an outer casing. Investigating further, she found an indentation on one side which seemed to have a lever attached. She pulled on the lever and the lid began to slide to one side, revealing a transparent inner receptacle. She leaned over and looked inside.

Lying in a prone position, dressed in elegant robes, was a body, floating in some kind of gaseous mist. Its eyes were tightly closed. She noticed the chamber was beginning to illuminate. Without knowing why, Marli crossed to the other sarcophagus and found another lever, and opened that one as well. Again, it began to illuminate. Then her telepathic sense became almost overloaded, bombarded with language and imagery. She sat between the two caskets, concentrating, her hands over her ears and her eyes tightly shut. Whatever was in the caskets was trying to communicate with her. She was eventually able to translate the gist of what was being said.

'We have been waiting for you to come to us. There is little time!'

# PLANET EARTH

In Port Lar, O'Reilly was relieved that he had managed to divert the attention of the fishermen away from a confrontation. He returned to his car and decided to head around the bay. As he drove up the north side, he noticed some traffic lights which seemed to be on 'red.' There was a long line of other cars waiting there. He got out of his vehicle and approached the driver in front, asking, 'What's going on?'

The driver replied. 'They're not letting anyone along here. Dunno what it is all about, been stuck here for ages!'

O'Reilly got out his mobile and called the station. 'What's happening in the bay? There's a massive queue here!'

The sergeant on duty replied, 'Where the hell have you been? Tell them all to turn round and go back. We've got to keep the bay road clear. There's a suspected explosive device in the water. They think it must be an old World War Two bomb or something. Anyway there's army personnel all over the place. Can you sort it out at your end?'

'Oh shit, that's all we need!' he replied as he reached for his blue light and stuck it flashing on the roof of his car. He then directed all the cars away from the scene and urged them to get to safety.

He then drove along the Prom to where a number of Land Rovers were parked. There was also a large black van with the letters ESS on the side. He parked next to them and knocked on the door of the van, which was promptly opened by a tall man with silver hair, dressed in combat gear.

'I am Detective O'Reilly of the local police. Who is in charge here?

'Ah, yes we have been expecting you, the name is Jonathan Holt, Major Jonathan Holt.'

'What's going on?' inquired O'Reilly.

'Well we were hoping that you could enlighten us on that, old man. What do you know of this boy Ben Ericson?'

'I know he's just a local kid with a few problems at the moment, why?'

'I think he's having more problems than you think. We suspect he's involved in something far beyond his control. We have been tracing him and his father's activities for some time now.'

The major did not pull any punches.

'We also think that his father was developing some sort of weapon. There are signs of extreme energies having been emitted over there,' he pointed towards the Emerald Rocks.

'I find this highly unlikely, Major. I know this kid.'

'Well, you had better take a look at some of this data,' replied the major, leading O'Reilly towards the back of the van which was lined with a huge array of very high tech equipment.

He asked a seated assistant to display a graph of the seismic activity in the area, which was far beyond the norm for this area. He also showed him transcripts from various tracking stations around the world, notifying him of the trajectory of some kind of energy source which seemed to have come from beyond the Earth, and was focussed upon a point near the Emerald Rocks. 'You must understand, Detective, that as yet we can find no explanation for these readings, and we would very much appreciate your cooperation.'

'Yes, Major, of course. Absolutely. There are a couple of things I would need to look into first, but then I can give you complete assistance.'

'Yes, yes we need you to maintain calm in the town. The last thing we need is any publicity. For the moment let's make them all think there's an unexploded WW2 bomb being removed.'

O'Reilly was utterly taken aback, and very much out of his comfort zone.

'This is just beyond belief! How could it be Ben?' he thought, letting out an exasperated sigh. 'I'm going to get to the bottom of this,' he said to himself. 'Mrs Ericson, you have some explaining to do!'

He shouted back to the men assembled around the control vehicle.

'Back soon. Just going to check back with the station.'

He got into his car and made his way through the narrow streets to the local police station. Although it was late, the place was completely lit up. He parked his car on a side street and slammed the door shut. It had been raining hard and there was a brisk wind blowing debris across the road. Kicking it out of the way, he entered the station, where he met the local bobby. Andy looked up from the front desk.

'You took your time, mate! I've been trying to get hold of

you for two hours!' Andy didn't care much for O'Reilly. He preferred to deal with his uniformed colleagues, believing detectives to be arrogant and difficult to deal with.

'Anyway, now you ARE here, what's the position with the military?'

'Seems there's some sort of unexploded WW2 bomb, they are busy assessing the situation.'

Andy looked peeved. 'And just what has 'Control' told us we are supposed to do about that?' he asked sarcastically.

'Bombs for Christ sake!' he said, shaking his head. 'I've practically got a riot going on down at the Fisherman's Arms.'

Steven, the most junior constable, was making the tea in the back. Overhearing the conversation, he suddenly piped up. 'There's been a telephone call saying there's an Audi Quattro parked across the farm gate up on Briar Hill.'

Andy shook his head. 'Yes Steven, let's not forget the really serious issues!' he said sarcastically.

Steven was now in full flow. 'And Old Bill Rogers is doing his nut. Seems he can't get through with his tractor to get the sheep off the hill, and there's a bike in the hedge AND ...'

Sergeant Andy cut him off. 'Concentrate on the tea, Steven.' He grimaced toward O'Reilly, 'Got a right one there,' he whispered

Andy was juggling with the responses to several incidents. The stormy weather had caused power cables to come down and there was some local flooding. Various vehicles were parked in places where they shouldn't be, and now the military had arrived to deal with an unexploded bomb.

'It's all kicking off, mate. All hands on deck so to speak. Given all this, I could have done without Mrs Ericson telling me her son has gone missing!'

These events suddenly lined up for O'Reilly. 'Hang on a minute! There's an Audi Quattro up Briar Hill, a bike in a hedge and Mrs Ericson's son is missing?'

'Sensible of you to go for the most important issues. Blimey, mate, get a grip!' Ignoring his sarcasm, O'Reilly said, 'Look, Sergeant, I'm going to deputise young Steven here to work with me for all of the next day.'

'What! You're joking!'

Andy was just about to ask 'Just what gives you the authority to ...' when the phone rang. The sergeant heard the crisp military tones of, 'Hello, this is Major Holt, I am just ringing to ensure that you are giving us your full cooperation.' Without replying, Andy put the phone down.

Andy was stumped, 'God help us. Well, Stevie boy, it looks like you have just been promoted from tea boy for the day. Go get your jacket lad!'

Steve's face lit up, 'Great! Thanks, Sarge.'

O'Reilly led the junior to his car and they drove off up to Briar Hill. The rain was pouring down and the road was covered in debris. Streams were overflowing and spilling into the road.

'Hold on tight, Steven, it's going to be a bit of a bumpy ride. Let me know if you can see anything out of the ordinary from your side. I can hardly see through this bit of the windscreen!'

The windscreen wipers swished backwards and forwards, struggling to clear the torrential rain off the screen. The car was rocked by the force of the wind howling off the sea.

Suddenly Steven shouted out, 'There, there on the hill, isn't that an Audi?'

O'Reilly slammed on the brakes and came to a sudden halt, almost colliding with a dilapidated stone wall. 'Sorry about that,' said O'Reilly, gathering his wits.

'Right, young fellah. Get up there and see what's what. If you see anything odd, don't do anything, just wait until I get back, okay?

'But it's raining, I'll get soaked!'

'Welcome to police work, lad. Now off you go. Remember to call in if you see anything unusual and don't forget your torch!'

Steven got out of the car and stumbled up the road towards the Audi. The beam from his torch lit the way and shone murkily through the mist. When he reached it he was surprised to find that the door was open and he looked inside. There were a few cans of lager, some fishing tackle and an old wax jacket. He searched through the pockets and found a wallet.

'Strange that someone has left their wallet,' he thought.

He scanned the contents and found a driving licence. He recognised the photo immediately.

'Hmm, Mr Toole, now what could you be up to tonight eh?' His curiosity stirred.

He reached for his walkie talkie and tried to get a signal.

'PC Steven Ward here, over.' He tried again. 'PC Steven Ward here, over.'

There was a crackling sound from the receiver but no audible voice.

Meanwhile, O'Reilly headed for the Ericson house. He swerved into the driveway and hastily made his way to the entrance. The front door was wide open. He looked around the house and called out. 'Mrs Ericson! Mrs Ericson!

O'Reilly here! We need to have a word!'

There was no answer. He checked all the downstairs rooms and made his way upstairs. He could see a light in one of the bedrooms and he could hear a whimpering voice. He pushed the door open and saw Grace on the floor weeping hysterically. She barely noticed him.

'He's gone, he's gone, I'm never going to see him again!'

O'Reilly grabbed a blanket and put it round her shoulders. She turned and looked at him. Her eyes were swollen with tears and she seemed to be shaking uncontrollably.

'It's going to be alright,' he said, giving her a comforting hug.

She clung onto him.

'It's not, everything's never alright!'

'Just calm down a little, Grace, while I call Amy.' He searched his pockets for his mobile and found her number. She answered immediately.

'Hello, Nurse Amy Rosser here, what's the problem?'

'It's O'Reilly here. Amy, can you get the Ericson house? It's about Grace.'

'No problem, I'll be there in ten minutes. How's Ben?'

'That's the problem. We just don't know. I'll fill you in when you get here.'

O'Reilly led Grace down to the kitchen and put on the kettle.

'I am so glad you are here,' said Grace.

'Look, Mrs Ericson, can I call you Grace?'

'Yes, what is it? Has something happened to Ben?'

'I don't know, I'm hoping you can help me with that.' He paused for a moment. 'Look Grace, you are going to have to trust me, and tell me everything you know.'

He looked at her with a serious expression. She looked back at him with wild staring eyes. It was more than she could cope with right now.

'How can I help?' she asked, taking a comforting sip of the tea.

'Perhaps we could go back and start at the beginning of all this. Can you tell me what Yan was really up to all that time?

'Oh God, yes, yes of course. Yan talked all the time about the Blue Men. He was obsessed by them.'

'Excuse me, Blue Men! Not the Blue Men legends again. What do you know about the weapon?'

'Weapon?! There was never any talk about a weapon!'

O'Reilly looked confused. 'This is all getting a bit too much. I've got the ESS Military Unit telling me that Yan was connected with some kind of weapon hidden in the Emerald Rocks. But all you can talk about is the Blue Men? Has everyone gone mad? And where does Ben fit in all this?'

At that moment his radio began to beep. 'PC Steven Ward here. Over.'

O'Reilly answered, 'O'Reilly here, anything to report, Steven? Over.'

'Yes sir, I think the Audi belongs to Mr Tool but he's nowhere to be seen. I think he might have hit a cyclist, because there's a bike in a mangled state on the road in front. Over.'

O'Reilly replied, 'Okay, check around the area. I'll get some backup and we will be there shortly. Over.'

At that moment Amy arrived at the house and O'Reilly met her at the door.

'Glad you are here, Amy. I have an incident on Briar Hill to deal with. I could say it's a fallen tree, but I would be lying. I have a feeling that things are connecting up in a way that puzzles me very much...' He broke off, as he noticed Grace staring intently at him.

'You have to take me there!' she cried.

'Okay, perhaps on the way you can start to tell some of the things you know!' The three of them left the house and got into his car. Once underway, he turned to Grace and asked, 'So. Do you know something about the Blue Men? Are they aliens? Did Yan see them? Am I right?'

Grace and Amy stared at him incredulously.

'Have you lost the plot, Mr O'Reilly? That Blue Man, Bluey thing is a legend.' Amy laughed

'I always thought so, but after today I am not so sure,' replied O'Reilly. Grace nodded slowly, staring ahead into the darkness.

# PLANET NEON

Quite by accident, Marli had walked into the tomb of the Great Saviours, Gathine and Tostare. She had a little knowledge of how they had heroically combined their intellects within the Directive, which then became vastly superior in its capabilities. It was able to construct the dome and save Seronia as a direct result. She could feel their identities reaching out to her with a power and clarity that was overwhelming. This was impossible and unbelievable. The experience began to intensify, until finally she could understand them clearly.

'WE ARE ONE MIND,' was the first clear 'message', followed by a vast array of images that she found hard to process.

At that point their identities seemed to approach her directly. A force that was irresistible began to inhabit her body and mind. It was so powerful that she had no choice but to succumb to its will.

In the 'sphere' there was a great deal of activity, as the 'V' transition had begun. Pedan was frantically monitoring the alignment of the quantum probe. He was trying to ignore the frantic gesturing of Mi, who was now hysterically shouting at him from behind the barriers.

The Mahon, followed by the Supreme Council, entered

the room. They took their positions on various raised platforms in an antechamber. There was a moment of silence, and then a high-pitched whine began to resonate around them. An image became visible within the centre of the chamber. It was a swirling vortex, and in the centre could be seen the image of another world.

# PLANET EARTH – BRIARS HILL

O'Reilly, Grace and Amy had lapsed into silence in the car. Everything seemed to have veered beyond reason. As they approached Briar Hill, they could see PC Ward in the gloom, walking back down towards them. They could see someone else with him. As they came closer they recognised that it was Tooley. He seemed to be limping badly and fell repeatedly. O'Reilly met them on the road. Tooley recognised him and said, looking rather sorry for himself, 'I've never been quite so glad to see coppers before!'

'Well done, PC Ward. Right Mr Tool I want a word with you!' cried O'Reilly, bundling him into the car.

As soon as they did, Tooley began to shout. 'No, no! You've got to help Ben! He's gone over to the Rocks,' he ranted. 'There's something really weird going on. If you don't help him Ben could drown. He's gone down the shaft!'

'Oh my poor Ben!' screamed Grace. 'Tooley how could you let him go down there?!' O'Reilly looked anxious. 'I had better go and investigate up there. Amy, please take care of Mr Tool.' He instructed Steven to stay with them and wait for back up. He went to the back of his car and grabbed a rope and a powerful torch.

'Yes sir, right okay,' Steven was enjoying all this action.

'I'm coming too,' insisted Grace, following him up the hill.

They made it up to the shaft and looked down into the hole.

'Oh, I can hear the rumble of the sea down there. The tide's coming in, so if Ben's down there we had better be quick.'

He secured the rope to a large post and scrambled down onto the overhang. He called up to Grace, 'Grab the rope and I'll catch you.'

She gripped the rope and despite her fear edged her way down. She felt O'Reilly grab her and help her over the overhang and down to the floor. He shone the torch down the length of the shaft.

'This place used to be used for smuggling. No wonder Tooley knew about it.'

Grace replied, 'Yes, I have been here before. Yan's dinghy is somewhere near the entrance. He used to leave it here when he was doing the surveys.' She had got her breath back.

'What exactly was your husband doing, Grace? Who was he really working for?' It seemed as good a time as any to ask those awkward questions.

'He was doing a geological survey for the Institute of Physical Research, but he was also researching marine gastropods.'

'What does that mean?' O'Reilly's knowledge of marine biology was minimal.

'There are gastropods, mussels and snails of some very interesting species around here, particularly the luminescent varieties. Some of them have remarkable environmental resistance. I know that Yan was fascinated by a particular one.' She suddenly stopped herself mid-flow and took a deep breath. 'I just realised, Ben was studying these very species at university. He was very keen to know all about them. In fact, he was looking for Yan's old notes just the other day!'

'I'm getting very confused here. The only mussels I like are the ones served up boiled with a bowl of chips!'

She ignored his attempt at levity and continued. 'He was talking a lot about terrestrial molluscs. Yes, I remember now, he was studying one group that seemed to have remained in a unique state of evolution. They think it's possible that spores of them in their nascent state might have been brought by a meteor that landed here. I think they are called Ellobidae. In fact, there is a colony of them in the Emerald Rocks.'

'Keep going, Grace, think. What else do you know?'

'Well, sometimes when there is a lot of activity, the water becomes a kind of bluish, violet colour, but it's thought that it's caused by the minerals that the rocks contain metamorphosed basalts and the like, why?'

O'Reilly looked more confused than ever, however, he was hearing what seemed to be an honest scientific opinion from Grace and didn't detect that she was covering up anything. 'I hate to ask this, but what do you think happened to your husband?'

She sat down on the rocky ledge and put her head in her hands. 'I just don't know. He had some fanciful notions, and he was fascinated by the local Blue Man legends. Maybe he just went too far in some direction I don't understand.'

O'Reilly didn't want to waste any more time.

'We need to get going, look at the sea!' he said, pointing to the opening of the cave. The water was now lapping over the far edges. He thought to himself, 'Where the hell is he?'

Just as they were about to drop down further, they realised that the water had come up too far.

'It's no good, we can't reach him from here. We will have to go back. The water will get far too deep in the tunnels.'

He put his arm around her and guided her back along the corridor of the shaft.

'Maybe, we could go up to the Point, there's a good view from there right across the bay,' suggested Grace

'Good idea, quick, there's not a lot of time.'

As they walked along the corridor up to the first level O'Reilly spotted something in a crevice. As they looked closer it became obvious that they were parts of a human skeleton.

Grace shrieked, 'Oh my God what is it?'

O'Reilly tried to calm her, 'Whatever it is, it's been there a hell of a long time. I'll have to get forensics down here to investigate another time. Come on, we've got to go.'

As they finally made their way out of the shaft they could see PC Ward waving frantically at them.

'What now?' thought O'Reilly.

# BEN

Ben was tossed out of the boat as it spun in the whirlpool. The vortex dragged him downwards beneath the waves. He thought he must have blacked out because he came too lying on the floor of an underground cavern. It was dimly lit by what seemed to be some kind of strange aura in the distance. He began to shiver and feel very cold as his wet clothes stuck to his skin. He took several deep breaths and tried to move, grimacing as he felt a sharp pain in his thigh. With all the effort he could muster he forced himself to stand up, and looked around. The only way out seemed to be in the direction of the light that seemed to be glowing in the distance. Forcing himself forward, he staggered unsteadily towards it.

As he got closer to the light, he was aware that it had some kind of humanoid shape. Although he found it difficult to focus his eyes on it, he was drawn to it, and felt no fear. Although he could physically see the image, he wondered whether he was seeing something which was not of this world at all. His heart began to beat faster and he felt a sense of unease.

He called out, 'What are you?'

There was no reply. It seemed to be beckoning him to follow. With a great sense of trepidation he placed one foot in front of the other and found himself following the 'shape'. The ground beneath him began to feel as if it was disappearing. However, he was still moving along. He looked around and there was only empty space. Again he called out, 'Who are you, what do you want with me?'

Then he heard what seemed to be a familiar voice. 'Ben.'

He looked up, and sensed someone or something that he knew, or had once known. Although what was happening was beyond his comprehension, he was happy to submit to the will of this strange force. Slowly, a bluish beam of light approached, and eventually surrounded him. Then he understood what was being asked of him.

Calmly he placed his hand in the pocket of his jacket. He could feel the shape of the Rosanthrocae mollusc there. Closing his hand around it he lifted it out of his pocket and into the light. He then closed his eyes and stood very still. The little mollusc was cradled in his palm. It felt like nothing he had ever felt before.

It began to vibrate, and then its shell slowly opened, exposing the fleshy interior. As he stared down at it, it began to radiate a rainbow of colours before releasing thousands of little spores that drifted upwards. It was a moment of utter beauty and tranquillity. Ben was mesmerised by the iridescence, and felt only joy and wonder. It was an overwhelming, overpowering experience. His consciousness felt as though it was expanding. He was being released from his earthly anxieties and drifting into a state of bliss. He wasn't sure if he was dead or alive.

The next thing he could remember was being back in the little dinghy. He grabbed the oars and began rowing. He had no idea of the direction he was going. He began to giggle and then this turned into laughter, his whole body convulsing uncontrollably. He just seemed not to have a care in the world. He hadn't felt like this since he was a child.

Then he felt the little dinghy begin to rise up, as if propelled from below. Smoothly it began to cruise forward.

# THE POINT

Major Holt was trying to make contact with Detective O'Reilly on the radio. Young PC Ward overheard the message.

'O'Reilly, get yourself here immediately, over.'

'PC Steven Ward here. Detective O'Reilly has left the vehicle in search of Ben Ericson, over.'

'Well, PC Steven Ward. There's a major event taking place down here. Find him and get to safety, over.'

Steven was taken aback, it all sounded very serious. He wasn't sure what to do. Fortunately, he could see two people were approaching. He breathed a sigh of relief as he recognised O'Reilly and Grace. He rushed out of the car to meet them.

'There's been an urgent message sir! They said something is happening in the bay!'

'Ok, young fellah, calm down. We'd better head for the Point.'

They decided to use the Audi, as it was the fastest vehicle. They all clung on as it sped along the narrow twisty lanes towards a landmark called 'Blue Point'. From there it was possible to see the complete crescent of the bay and the Emerald Rocks. On a fine night it was a very popular spot as it was possible to experience a genuine dark sky, free of street lights. The stars would be evident in all their glory. If there was a full moon this would illuminate the waters of the bay, it was a spectacular viewpoint.

As they approached the Point, there seemed to be a lot of vehicles gathered there.

'Strange, wonder what all the commotion is?' thought O'Reilly.

Then, as they turned into the carpark, something totally unexpected happened.

# PLANET NEON – THE PORTAL

The Mahon and the Supreme Councillors were still standing on platforms in the area that encircled the portal. This was where the vortex emanated now that the 'V' programme had been activated. The quantum probe was now focussed. This was a dangerous development, as there had not been a thorough assessment of its consequences. To initiate it in haste like this, with no real certainty that it was viable or stable, could be disastrous. They all stood in silence, mesmerised by the whirling mass in the centre of the chamber, which was spinning faster and faster.

As they watched, waiting for something to materialise, they were disturbed by Marli walking slowly towards them. She had an utterly blank expression on her face. The entire Supreme Council turned in her direction. The Mahon was the first to speak.

'Upon what authority do you enter the inner sanctum?'

'My authority is beyond that of yours' she replied calmly.

The council members exchanged glances. No one had ever dared to challenge the Mahon.

'For whom do you speak!' asked the Mahon, somewhat agitated.

Marli edged towards the assembled circle, her eyes wide and staring. Pedan could hardly believe what he was seeing, but took the opportunity to make adjustments to the probe. He signalled surreptitiously to Mi, who was also witnessing Marli's intrusion.

Suddenly, Marli looked up into the spherical frustum of the orb. She raised her arms. With an almighty crack, the wall began to fracture above them.

The Mahon, seeing that the fissures were lengthening rapidly, froze in disbelief.

'What are you doing, fool? You will kill us all!' he shouted, enraged.

'This is your moment of truth,' Marli intoned clearly.

As one, the Council rushed towards her, but came up against some kind of force field. They were no match for this entity. The Mahon attempted to summon the Directive.

It was futile, as the Directive had moved into evolve mode in order to protect itself. Marli was representing a power that it could not comprehend. The resulting effect was that all systems in the city began to shut down. The city was now paralysed.

Meanwhile, Mi saw her chance, as the trooper droids were disengaged from the Directive. She slipped out of her cell and ran to where Quilliam was being held. As she approached the room she could see Pedan in the way.

'Get away from him!' she hissed, lunging at him.

'Stop Mi! If I don't disconnect the probe we will lose him forever!'

She stood back with uncertainty.

'Be quick, the sphere is collapsing,' she waited.

This was the most anxious moment of her life. There in front of her was her son, but she had to trust that Pedan would do the right thing. She held her breath.

Pedan made a final adjustment and then slowly detached the probe from Quilliam.

His body began to shudder and come back to life.

Mi put her hand on Quilliam's head, tears rolling down her cheek.

At that moment he regained consciousness. He opened his eyes and looked around.

'Where am I?' his speech was slurred.

'You are safe, but we have to go.' Pedan and Mi lifted him off the table together.

'Marli, Marli where is she?' asked Quilliam.

'She is here, but, well I don't' know, something is happening with her. It's all very confusing,' said Mi, shaking her head.

'I'm not leaving without her,' Quilliam was adamant

'Okay, we will have to be quick, maybe if we go this way,' They led him to a room adjacent to the inner chamber of the orb.

Marli was still standing in the centre of the sphere, the portal was swirling around in front of her. Then thousands of little spores seemed to emerge from the centre, swirling in incredible colours. As the spores floated upwards towards the now fractured sphere, they began to escape into the outside atmosphere and dispersed evenly all around the city.

Then there was a moment of calm as the portal closed.

As Quilliam and Mi entered the room, Marli collapsed. Quilliam rushed over to her and picked her up, feeling her body lifeless in his arms.

# PLANET EARTH – THE BOMB

O'Reilly, Grace, Amy, Tooley and PC Ward all stood at the top of the cliff. As they looked across the bay they could see that all the military boats had fled the scene. There was something happening around the rocks. The ground around them seemed to shake and the sea seemed to be boiling. There was a huge explosion, drawing several screams of panic from the crowd. Everyone was looking for somewhere safe to hide as someone shouted, 'Bomb!'

Down in the harbour there was pandemonium. The military had ordered an evacuation of the entire vicinity, including the locals who had gathered in the Fisherman's Arms.

'Get yourselves to high ground, fast!' Someone shouted as several soldiers ushered them out of the pub.

'What, what about the boats? shouted Frank

'We have done all we can. No time to lose, for God's sake move!'

Frank looked out to sea, and noticed there was a massive looking wave rising around the Emerald Rocks.

'C'mon, everyone, get out as fast as you can. Billy, get the land rover!'

They all dashed to the vehicles and sped up the road. All the boats in the bay were bobbing around, and some were breaking away from their moorings and slamming into the side of the quay.

Already, there seemed to be quite a huge swell, driving water over the promenade itself. Second by second, the waves were gaining energy and thrashing the wall. In the distance it looked like the water around the rocks was still boiling. The rocks themselves seemed to be shaking as a great wave completely enveloped them. The rocks began to crumble and disappear underneath the water. The wave towered up and continued in its menacing journey towards the shore.

With the news of the 'bomb', the buildings near the shore had fortunately been successfully evacuated. Shelters had been erected on top of the cliff and blankets and refreshments were being handed to the evacuated villagers. They were shocked and shaken but hadn't come to any harm. They watched in horror as the enormous wave unleashed its destructive forces, battering the shoreline and destroying anything in its path.

Tooley was standing at a point where he could peer right over the cliff. He watched in horror as the huge wave gathered momentum and swelled ever higher on its way to the shore. Squinting his eyes, he suddenly picked out a shape in the water.

'What's that on top of the waves?' he shouted over to O'Reilly.

'Oh my God! It's not possible!' The blood drained from his face.

'What's wrong?' Grace tugged at him.

By this time Amy was standing next to them and they all stared in utter disbelief.

They could clearly see the crest of the wave, reaching at least forty feet high, heading rapidly towards the shore. Carried along on the very top, they could make the outline of a little dinghy, with a figure inside it.

Tooley suddenly burst out with, 'It's Ben, it's f ... ing Ben, what is he doing?'

'No, no it can't be,' Grace screamed.

Amy put her arm around Grace.

Everyone rushed to see what all the commotion was about. Quick as a flash, Tooley made a dash for the Audi, followed by O'Reilly.

'Quick get in, if we go down to Neb we might be able to see where he lands.'

They sped down the road and headed for the 'Neb'. This was an outcrop at the head of a sandy bay near the dunes.

'I think that is where he is heading,' said Tooley.

'I don't think he is gonna make it.' O'Reilly was apprehensive.

'We can't give up on him.' Tooley was determined.

Ben meanwhile was deliriously euphoric. He had grabbed onto the sides of the dinghy and was riding the wave without a care in the world. The dinghy slipped down its crest and somehow remained upright as it rushed along. As the wave broke it swept up the beach with incredible ferocity. The boat seemed to skid along on its very crest and was propelled far into the sand dunes, finally coming to a standstill amongst a hump of seagrasses.

Tooley and Detective O'Reilly had now reached the top of the sand dunes.

'Now watch what this baby can do!' said Tooley.

He put the Audi into four-wheel drive and slammed up the first dune.

'Watch what you are doing!' said O'Reilly, finding himself momentarily airborne. Then Tooley pointed. 'I think he might be over there.' He put the car into first gear and slid down the dune and onto the beach. Sand was flying everywhere as it rocketed along.

'Stop, you maniac. I think I can see something!' shouted O'Reilly. He could see an upturned boat, but no sign of Ben. 'Oh my God, I've got a bad feeling about this,' he muttered. Tooley jumped on top of the bonnet and scoured the area.

'I can see something, over there, quick.'

Tooley had spotted Ben. They ran toward him, to find him lying on his back, unconscious.

Tooley shouted loudly, 'Is he dead?'

O'Reilly knelt down beside him and listened to his chest.

'He's breathing, let's get him back.'

They carefully carried him onto the back seat of the car and sped off to the hospital. Grace was waiting in the A&E.

'I can't lose him. I can't lose him,' she was sobbing. Ben was placed on a trolley and wheeled away. O'Reilly went up to Grace and put his arm around her. 'He's gonna be alright just ...' He paused 'Somehow I know it.'

# PLANET NEON – NOVARIA

As the ceiling of the sphere had shattered, the Mahon and the Councillors were left stranded on one of the elevations. They were helpless as they watched the spores drift higher and higher into the dome.

It was not at all the result that they had expected, in fact it was the antithesis of all their computations. The spores which should have regenerated the dome were now beginning to destroy it.

'Follow me,' the Mahon ushered the councillors to follow him. Some followed, some were reticent and remained. The Mahon shouted back at them, 'You fools, follow me or face certain death.' But they felt they could not trust him. To their horror he exited the room and sealed the door behind him.

The Mahon took a small entourage with him to an emergency assembly area. The rest of the councillors retreated to a small chamber at the side of the orb.

The Mahon signalled for the transport shuttle. They boarded and sped down into the depths of the city, to the NS1. This was the Novaria holding area. It was a top secret project and very few knew of its existence. The Novaria was a celestial spacecraft. It was being prepared for launch. It had been conceived in secret and initiated by the Directive.

It would be an Ark, in the event of another Catastrophe. There were many technicians and various personnel busily transporting items onto platforms which were then being hoisted onto the craft. They had rehearsed this procedure many times, but now it was for real.

The Novaria was an amazing construction. The outer shell was made from a trithiane, with a gleaming translucence. It looked like an enormous gyroscope. Its modular design allowed it to assume many different configurations. This would enable it to resist all manner of cosmic forces and pressures. As soon as it was activated the inner body began to vibrate while the outer ring began to spin. It would have to reach optimum velocity within seconds if it was to be able to escape the gravitational pull of the planet. Time was of the essence.

The Mahon boarded the craft and immediately assumed control. The councillors who had stayed with him went to their command positions. Everything was set and ready. Within seconds the craft began to hover and ascend through the parapet. Suddenly there was an enormous vibration which seemed to shake the city. It began to rise further, and then transformed into a cone in order to make its launch. On gaining the outer atmosphere, it assumed the shape of a huge dart and was effortlessly propelled onwards. Once released from its terraqueous state it effortlessly glided into an orbit. It created a crescent shape of charged tribane particles in its wake. The glittering rainbow of particles then diffused and in an instant it was gone. All that was left was a shining afterglow.

It was an engineering masterpiece.

Back in the orb, Marli was beginning to stir.

'What's happening, where am I?' she asked, utterly disorientated.

'I don't know, but it's truly amazing!' said Quilliam.

She looked up and saw that the dome was beginning to disappear.

'Are we going to die?' she asked, holding onto him tightly.

Quilliam began to blink and rubbed his eyes as he adjusted to the clarity of the light.

'Look!' said Marli.

He looked into the distance and he could see the Ariane Mountains. Looking closer, he could identify individual hills and make out the lush green pasturelands. He looked up and he could see the sun and its moons. No longer contained within the dome, the air was sweet and smelled divine.

'What just happened?' asked Marli.

'I have no idea!'

Meanwhile, Pedan, still at the command aperture, had an idea.

'If I reinterpret the language frequency and instigate a syntactic alignment then perhaps ... hmmmm.'

'Pedan, what are you doing?' cried Mi, highly distressed.

'Have you noticed that we still seem to be breathing ok?' said Pedan.

'Yes, but we might be just surviving on the residual air. How long do we have?'

Mi looked across at Pedan, who was adjusting some controls.

'What's going on, what have you done?' she stared at him.

'Me? Absolutely nothing.'

'Whatever is that?' said Mi.

Pedan looked at her for a moment, then said, 'You must take shelter.'

'No, I'm staying here, whatever happens we will face it together.'

Pedan smiled. In her vulnerability she was beautiful.

# THE THARMENIAN ADVANCE

In the labyrinth there was a place called the Dream Chamber, a place of great significance to the Tharmenians. Hundreds of years previously, some unusual drawings had been made there. It was thought that they had been made by the ancestral dream makers. They still looked remarkably clear despite their obvious age. They were very complex, filling the whole ceiling of the chamber. The most prominent feature was a circle which encompassed two moons and a sun, and within the circle were many different representations of people. There were symbols that seemed to represent mountains along with crudely drawn pictures of dwellings, wavy lines and fish symbols. There was also a strange looking creature which resembled a unicorn, looking up towards a group of stars.

For many years the people had drawn all kinds of conclusions about it. Some felt a strange magical connotation, for others it was simply a fable of their creation. The symbol of the unicorn seemed to be a reference to a mythical creature. The chamber was treated as a holy sanctum.

It was customary for the 'Baliya' to conduct a blessing ceremony there at the beginning and end of the winter and summer quat. He would be accompanied by various disciples. They would spend several days and nights in the chamber, chanting rituals followed by discourses, meditation and sleep.

One such ceremony had just occurred, but it had had disturbing consequences for one of the disciples, named Amos. Amos had lived in the close community of the Baliya from a young age. He had a unique aura and it was felt that he needed guidance in order to understand his 'gifts'. He seemed to have prophetic abilities, and often had visions which had on many occasions come true.

On the eve of the winter quat ceremony Baliya and his disciples had entered the Dream Chamber as usual. It would be a night of ritual, contemplation and meditation. However, something began to disturb Amos. He began to babble incoherently.

'The stars are raining down, raining down!' he said, repeating it over and over again

'What's happening to Amos?' The other disciples became worried.

'The 'Rarwhal,' is calling me, calling me,' he cried, naming the mythical unicorn creature.

He became more and more agitated.

'The city, the city is awakening, we must go and bring them home.'

He became feverish and delirious. The Baliya realised that something highly auspicious was happening. Then they looked up at the ceiling of the chamber, and noticed that the paintings had become animated. The chamber was filled with light. They began to have a shared vision, something which had never happened before. There was a feeling of great urgency.

Eventually, they began to regain their senses but Amos was different; he could not be consoled. The Baliya understood that Amos was now the chosen one, and would lead them. They had to obey the calling and seek out this new destiny. It would be the greatest journey of their lives.

It was fortuitous that there were thousands of Tharmenians making camp in the sacred valley. This being the fourth quat was also the time of the blooming of the Rosanthrocae. The air was filled with excitement.

This was always the most holy of gatherings. The high point would be the ceremonial procession to the dell where they would receive a blessing.

Everyone was preoccupied with the preparations. It would be a colourful and wonderful spectacle. They were busy dressing themselves in all kinds of adornments. They would look resplendent in their highly ornate headdresses and body paint.

As was customary, they began to take their places for the great procession. However, the Baliya stood on the high ledge. This was highly unusual. As they gathered beneath, all were commanded to be silent. Then the Baliya began his decree. 'You must go quickly, it is the time, our brother Amos will guide you to the great upland. The journey will be long and you must go with hearts of courage to bring about a great change.'

Everyone was stunned and there was much trepidation. The Baliya, then asked one of his disciples to bring the sacred ceremonial staff. This he raised above his head and it directed a glowing beam of light in the direction of Seronia. This lit the path they were to follow. They would cross the great plain and ascend the plateau.

It was a most foreboding sight to see so many Tharmenians leave the sanctity of their lands, with no idea about what was ahead.

The Baliya remained at the dell along with the more senior Partisans. He had to prepare himself.

Amos would lead them to the north side of the plateau. He stood in awe as he looked out towards the city. To him it was an incredible sight. The vast shapes, the lights, the buildings themselves. The great conurbation was like nothing he had ever seen before. They made their way to the perimeter where they located the plinths. Gathering around, they began to chant their holy mantras and the sound echoed downwards, across the plateau and over the city.

'What is that?' Mi looked, terrified. Then she saw scores of Tharmenians silhouetted against an open horizon.

The spores that had emerged from the shattered fissures of the dome were heading in their direction. They produced an incandescence which illuminated the sky above them. Amos gave the order for them all to enter the city. They began a slow, deliberate rhythmic march.

Meanwhile something had disturbed Marli.

'I can hear something., she held her head in her hands. 'it's very strong ... I.

It wants to speak!' she looked at Quilliam with wild staring eyes.

'What's wrong, what's happening to you?' Quilliam became very concerned

'It says that he wants to go, to be set free!' Instinctively she knew where the telepath was.

She ran down the corridor. Quilliam followed. She was heading for the crypt. She pushed the door open and ran over to the sarcophagi.

'What are they?' asked Quilliam as he stood back, utterly mystified.

'I think they are the forgotten ones. The Tharmenians have come for them.

We must do something to help them.'

'Let's push them into the hub on that transporter over there,' said Quilliam.

The transporter was a wheeled flat-bedded trolley. As sarcophagi seemed to be floating above the podiums, it was easy to turn them and direct them to the trolley.

'Where to now?' Quilliam asked, mystified.

'To the shuttle and then to the arena,' Marli replied. The sarcophagi were strangely weightless and they found it easy to push them along. It was easy enough to steady them as the shuttle sped to the floor of the great arena.

Finally, with all the strength they could muster, they pushed them through the exit point to the outside.

They had no idea what to expect next. Here they were face to face with the thousands of Tharmenians who were gathering there. At the sight of the two gleaming sarcophagi there was utter silence, then all the Tharmenians fell to their knees.

Amos came towards them. He stretched out his hands. Then there was a strange sound emanating from above them. They looked up and saw that there was a fantastic murmuration of the spores, swirling around in the sky and making all kinds of exotic patterns. Marli and Quilliam held their heads low. Everyone was silent. Quietly at first, they began chanting, rising in volume minute by minute.

The Tharmenians began to chant louder and louder. As one, they looked upwards and saw the two moons as they began to drift together, until there was a total eclipse. There was a sense of something utterly transcendent. It lasted for just a moment. Then, as the moons gradually separated, Amos instructed the Partisans to lift and bear the sarcophagi on their shoulders. The Tharmenians began their slow retreat. The cloud of spores seemed to follow them. Amos turned to Marli and Quilliam and said, 'Their souls are at peace now, we will take their mortal remains to a final resting place. This is the beginning of a new dawn.'

They watched as they retreated in the direction of Tharmenia in a steady and gracious manner. The lights from their torches gradually faded as they descended down into the great forest below, and then onwards across the plains. The sounds of their chanting gradually dissipated, and then they were gone.

The city of Seronia was still in a lockdown. There was very little that people could do. Many were stranded in the underground passageways, and unable to reach the safety of their pods. Some began to congregate in the great arena. Everyone was shaken by the spectacle of the Tharmenians. Now all they could do was wait.

Those that had gathered in the arena began to notice that the sky, which previously had been hidden by the dome, was beginning to reveal itself. As it did, rays of light from the red Neonian sun began to light up the structures. It was a different kind of light, far brighter than what they were used to. Then the sun began to sink behind a nebula of clouds. This created a prism that was deflected around the city. This was the first sunset that they had ever experienced, and everyone was transfixed.

The Seronians, however, were also left feeling bewildered. There was no Directive to guide them and the city was still shut down.

The light from the spores had also attracted the Calfarians. Many had entered the city from the Levels. There they found many forlorn looking Seronians, huddled together, in a very distressed state.

Immediately, they began to offer help. They guided them to the underwater pods, where they were able to shelter. The Calfarian people were sad to see their dilemma. The Seronians were humbled by their kindness.

Pedan and Mi were still in the orb.

'We must ask the Directive what to do,' said Mi.

'The Directive is in a state of excogitation. We must be patient,' said Pedan.

'But the people, they need help!'

Pedan looked down towards the arena and he could see that the people were now being assisted and helped by the Calfarians.

'I never thought a time would come when I would see such a thing.'

There seemed to be an army of Calfarians ushering people to safety and taking care of the desperate Seronians. Their acts of kindness were a testimony to their character.

Mi was suddenly overcome by what she saw. 'I feel so ashamed. How could we have maligned such kind and caring people?'

Pedan replied, 'There is much we have to change, but

there is one final thing that I must do.'

Mi turned to him. 'Are you really going to do that?' She had guessed what he was about to do.

'Yes, it is the future for us all.' And he wandered off.

Pedan made his way back to the orb where the Directive was housed. It was his intention to reinitialise the programmes which maintained the city, but the Mahon had beaten him to it. He had instructed that its data systems were to be taken and installed into the mainframe systems of the 'Novaria' craft. It now left the city systems paralysed, with Cora and everything else defunctioned.

Pedan sighed, 'No! It's too late, they have taken it!'

Then something began to stir in the motherboard. Pedan suddenly saw a flicker of something bright emanate from the housing. Suddenly, the room began to fill with light.

He stood in awe and was utterly perplexed by it. Then a voice rang out

'Etherea at your command!'

Pedan stood motionless as the voice continued, then an image of the Rarwhal was projected into the sky. It hung above the assembled crowds like an ethereal being. A strange and mystical sound seemed to envelope them.

A voice rang out from the sky itself.

'We are the Ethereans, here to serve all beings. We must all come together in peace for the good of all of our nations. We do so in honour of our dearly departed.'

Pedan knew this was a pivotal moment for everyone. There was a great deal of relief, particularly amongst the Seronian people. In their darkest hour, this new Etherean Directive would be their Saviour.

Over time, many changes came about. A new council

with representatives from each of the Domains was established. There was to be a new Dictum. They would be guided by Ethereal Law, which was sensitive to everyone's cultural identities.

The Seronians embraced this new diversity as it brought them new freedoms and opportunities to explore their entire planet.